# Read 'Em & Weep

A Handful of Stories About Unusual Players

Andrew Allen
Matthew J. Kolell
Catalino Tolejano, II
Patrick A Waldoch

Published by Authors Rising, LLC

**Published by**
**Authors Rising, LLC**
**Milwaukee, WI**
**www.authorsrising.com**

Cover photo by A. Weisensel
Cover layout by Darin Weisensel
Interior Design by A. Weisensel

ISBN-10: 0-9830746-0-7
ISBN-13: 978-0-9830746-0-1

This book is dedicated to all aspiring writers everywhere. If you want to be published, and are willing to work hard, listen to honest feedback, and help others, come see us. :)

-Authors Rising

Thanks to family & friends for their support and understanding, and my far-away fiancée for believing in me. Thanks also to all the authors who have inspired me with their stories, writing blogs, and hard work – from Jim Butcher, to the other guys in this book, and all the rest at AuthorsRising.com.

-Andrew Allen


Thank you to Sara for her love and support. Also to Andrew for putting this together and dealing with my procrastination.

-Matthew J. Kolell


I'd like to thank Andrew for bringing us together and driving this project to fruition. I'd also like to thank my wife, Carrie, for supporting me and allowing me to sit and stare at blank pages on a computer screen when I could have given her a modicum of the attention she deserved. And most of all, I'd like to thank my son CJ for being so excited to sit and bang on a keyboard that I couldn't help but want to join him!

-Catalino Tolejano, II


My thanks to the other Authors Rising & Andrew especially for envisioning this project. And to Tina for her love, support and proof-reading skills. (She caught more missing commas than everyone else combined!) My story is dedicated to the gamers and old friends that formed the foundation for the characters. Brian, Tag, Craig and Marcus our GM who conceived the Star Wars d6 sessions that birthed The Bootlegger, Marlene and her crew. (Even Timothy and the Bottle o' Rum made an appearance!) May the Regency live on anew.

-Patrick A. Waldoch

*CONTENTS*

# No Card Can Help You

# Poke Her

# Last Man Dying

# Honor Among Traitors

# No Card Can Help You

*Andrew Allen*

## Chapter 1
### Here's the Deal


I once had a "Texas Hold 'em for Dummies" deck of cards. Across the face of each card, it gave hints to help beginning players decide whether to fold early, or stay in to see the flop. On the King of Spades it might say, "bet on 10 of spades, or any Jack or higher" if you were one of the first to act, or, "any spade/any 9 or higher" if you were one of the last. You'd look at your other card and try to decide whether you play it smart—and do what they told you—or if you just had a hunch that *this* time you could beat the odds. Sure, in an ordinary situation, the 2-7 off-suit you'd been dealt might not be that great, but you're no ordinary guy... And what if the flop comes up 7-2-7 —you've seen it happen— and you'd let the chance for a big win pass you by...

A lot of the cards, however, just had one simple line:

"No card can help you."

If you've got this card, it doesn't matter what else you've got going for you — you might as well just give up.

Right then, I knew exactly how that felt.

We'd been sitting here in the car for almost 3 hours, parked on a moderately busy street on the East side of Milwaukee. It was late afternoon. Cars came and went from the parking spots often enough that, so far, it didn't seem like anyone would've taken much notice of us in our dark blue Chevy sedan. From here I could see both the bagel shop on the corner and a particular house that I'd been keeping my eyes on about two-thirds down the block.

Deuce -- named for the first car he'd stolen back when he was 13, a classic "little deuce coup" (and incidentally, also the first time he was apprehended ...and his first night spent in a holding cell... and thus the *last* car he'd ever stolen) -- had fallen asleep a little over an hour ago. He hadn't even woken up when I'd gotten out to put more change in the meter. I couldn't blame him, really... he worked nights, like most of us in the "Lonely Hearts" side of our organization, catering to the needs of our adult clientele. He did well, with his dark skin and the flamboyant attitude he affected; he drew those who wanted something a bit exotic, and were willing to pay extra for it. Quite a contrast to my normal role: the ruggedly handsome Spanish gentleman... with just enough rogue at the edges to add some excitement. We made a good team when we chose to. Today, though, this was all my show. As far as he was concerned, his part in this was over once he had gotten me here. He'd only agreed to stay around because he owed me. And, at least for the moment, he felt I still had a possible impact on his future advancement.

Not like I was that important, really -- but at least I had a seat at the table, so to speak. I handled special situations for the "enterprises of the heart" ... only a couple steps away from one of the 4 A-level bosses at the top of the whole organization. Deuce was always going to be one of those guys that was on the edges, running errands, working for others even when he wasn't serving as a joy-boy. He was still a good guy, and I had learned a long time ago you treat everyone with respect, no matter what their rank. But unlike Deuce, I had plans of my own.

Unfortunately, those plans didn't always work out. I'd had a string of bad luck lately, and as the tension grew with the Madame that oversaw our bordellos, I was almost out of my personal capital. She acted like she was some kind of royalty, and I was just there to serve her personal whims... excuse me if I didn't take to that role to well. I knew my role in the organization -- and there was a lot more to it than just being her lackey. But the "Queen of Hearts," if you will, just saw it as my refusal to accept her authority. (Yeah, I know, I use a lot of card & poker metaphors... great game, keeps the mind sharp and helps you learn to read people.) She'd been making my life increasingly difficult, and whittling down my responsibilities. In theory, my position reported directly to the boss in charge of our whole division, Mr. A. Corazon himself. Problem was, the top positions weren't Stateside. I'd never even met him. And she still outranked me -- just enough to be the one in charge of local affairs. She said she was just trying to make sure I didn't have "more than I could handle." I wasn't sure how much longer before she tried to take me out of the game completely -- and I wouldn't have the resources to fight back.

Which is why we were sitting in this car, trying to act natural, and waiting. Heh, I guess Deuce had that "act natural" thing spot-on at that point.

I watched someone leave the bagel shop, with a bag in their arms... but no, it was a guy, and he headed across the street to an old pickup. That wasn't our mark.

I still wasn't entirely sure about this whole idea. I'd heard from Deuce here that one of our escorts had been talking about a "friend" who was bringing in something new. Something that might not cleanly fit the established "lines of business" in our organization, which could spark a bit of a turf war.... "I jus' knew I'd better dump it on you pronto, Jack..." he had said, in his heavy not-quite-from-anywhere accent, "I likes to get noticed, but that'd be the kind of attention Deuce don't want noooo part of."

There was a delicate balance in our organization ... well ok, not *that* delicate, but at least a normal way of doing things. If this was big enough for people to risk upsetting that balance, then there was definitely cash to be made if I could get in on it somehow. And this "friend" wouldn't be high up enough to keep me out of it once I knew. But, of course, it all depended on who else she was involved with.

The safe bet here would be to pass on what I'd heard to others who were in a better position to act, and drop out of it. Just like Deuce was doing. But they'd act to turn the situation to their own advantage. If I took the time to get to know who and what this was all about, I might be able to use that to *my* advantage instead. If they were bringing new cash to the table, I might be able to get a piece of the action. We can't control the opportunities life puts before us, but it's up to us what we do with the hands we're dealt.

The Queen would be furious if she found out I was going behind her back -- but the potential payoff might be enough to get me back in the game without her looming over me.

It was a risky play on my part, if it worked at all. I had no idea yet who else I'd be up against.

"Deuce, wake up." I smacked him on the chest.

"Yeah, man, I'm up, I'm up... what?"

"Is that her?" A tall, beautiful girl with red hair and a dancer's body had just come out of the shop. She wore trendy jeans, and dark glasses hid her eyes from the morning sun. She was heading purposefully our way in a tired but graceful walk.

"That's her, that's her..." he smiled... "see, I told you she was gorgeous... and smart, watch out ...a classic '10' all the way, baby. "

She moved down the block towards the flop-house. Pausing on the sidewalk, she quickly looked around to see if anyone was watching, then went up the stairs and through the front door. It was almost comical to see someone so obviously used to being the center of attention suddenly decide to try to look "normal."

"Did you see that key detail, Deuce?"

"What.... her suddenly decidin' she didn' want nobody seeing her go in?" he guessed.

I smiled... "The door wasn't locked."

"Well, you found her. What's the play, Jack, my man?" Deuce had his hand on the door handle, ready to go.

This was it. I could cut out now, with only minor losses, and wait for the next opportunity... or I could go see what there was to see in that flop-house, with only Deuce to back me up. Sooner or later I'd have to take a risk if I wanted to win, and this was as good a bet as any. I looked over at Deuce, waiting expectantly. He probably wouldn't be so eager if he knew I was doing this without approval from the top. I shook my head...'No card can help you'... but I guess if you're almost out of chips, any two cards can play...

"Alright, I'm in."

## Chapter 2
### The Flop House

We got out of the car, and I checked the time remaining on the meter: seventeen minutes. Ought to be plenty for what I had in mind.

I was used to being noticed -- we all were in our line of business. Good looking & well-dressed in tailored suits (we all had suits in this organization), we stood out. We might not sport the diamond-studded Rolex's & tie-tacks of the high-rollers, or the piercings & funky hair to fit into the club scene... But we on the "romance-for-hire" side of things definitely made our suits look good.

What with Deuce being even more noticeable than I was, nondescript was out of the question. Instead, we were going for an easy confidence, like we belonged. At least that way we shouldn't raise any immediate alarms if the neighbors saw us.

We headed up the steps of the small two-story house, paused a moment on the porch as if we had rung the bell, and then Deuce nonchalantly opened the door. I stepped inside like I owned the place.

The door opened onto a small living room, with what was probably intended to be a "dining room" just beyond. A few pieces of decent furniture were arranged around the room -- pretty much what you'd expect to see in a normal home. The TV was on, which was good, and there was some sort of chunky beef stew in a bowl on the table in front of it.

The kitchen was visible though a doorway in the far wall, a hallway opened to the right off the living room, and a stairway on the left led to the second floor. I was guessing our mark was either down the hall, or else in the kitchen in back. I waved Deuce towards an area of the room where he wouldn't be immediately visible to either entrance, and then took a seat on the couch, watching the TV. The show didn't matter -- I picked out the reflections in a picture on the wall, and was able to keep a distorted eye down the hall by doing so.

I thought about eating the stew, but decided that would be taking things a bit too far. Besides, it looked like it was some kind of quick microwave thing. A bit odd... probably not her usual fare? In fact, now that I looked around the room, it didn't really seem like our mark fit in here. There was neither the style of someone who knew & cared, nor the disorder of someone who didn't.

I heard a flush. When the bathroom door opened a moment later, the picture's distorted reflection showed me a dark figure step out into the hallway. Time to play it smooth and confident.

I turned on the charisma, flashed my most charming smile, and looked up... just as another suit came walking out of the hallway.

He jumped when he saw me, clearly startled. I tried to hide my own moment of shock, and forced myself to look away calmly, towards the TV. What the hell!? I hadn't thought there'd be anyone else here. My pulse was racing, but I hoped his was, too -- and I told myself he was probably a lot more surprised than I was.

"I can't believe you actually watch this stuff" I said far more casually than I felt, looking back at him, and motioning towards the show. Trying hard to send out an "I belong" vibe.

"You with Anya?" he challenged questioningly... "She didn't say she was bringing anyone."

He looked at Deuce standing in the corner... I don't think he or I had noticed what Deuce's reaction had been -- but he looked at home now, acting as if he had been examining a picture on the wall. I don't think this guy knew what to make of us. Deuce just looked at me, and the newcomer followed his gaze.

I put a slightly amused expression on, leaned back, and let his question hang in the air for longer than he was comfortable with. Looking up at him, I picked out the telltale signs that told me what this suit was... expensive but conservative shoes, pressed shirt & tie... and the glint of way too many diamonds. His ring, his tie tack, his watch... I couldn't see any cuff links, but he clearly wasn't Lonely Hearts like Deuce & me. How did he connect to our mark? To 'Anya,' (apparently).

And *then* she stepped through the kitchen doorway, with a bowl of strawberries in hand -- and I realized she wasn't just the "friend" of an escort. She was one of us. I'd definitely seen her involved in work in one of our houses. Something definitely didn't fit.

"What was that?" she replied, responding to his overheard question. She looked up from the bowl and stopped in surprise as she saw me, a strawberry halfway to her mouth. Some sort of partial recognition crossed her face, as she demanded "Who are you?"

I looked from her back to our mystery guest (or was that me at this point?)... "Not exactly," I finally answered him, and I could feel the uncertainty on his part as I regained control of the situation. Then turning towards where she still stood holding the strawberries, I smoothly said "it's Jack, don't you remember me, Anya?"

"Anya?" she said, and then louder, "Anya!"

Wait, ...what? So much for being smooth -- this really wasn't going quite as well as I'd thought, after all.

Our redhead finally looked around, and saw Deuce still standing over in the corner... "Deuce?" she questioned, "what are *you* doing here?" Sure, *him* she knew.

He looked from her, to the guy, to me, to her again... "Hey, Deena..."

And then, of course, I heard yet *another* person, starting down the stairs towards us. I knew our mark couldn't be doing this alone, *why* hadn't it occurred to me there'd be others here?

"Denari, what is it? No need to raise your voice" -- the lower tone of a slightly older woman, but actually not so old as she came around the corner. *This* must be Anya... "who are these people, Jack?"

Again ...what? How did she know who I...?

"We were just about to find out," replied... um... he must be another 'Jack,' I guess? Now wait a minute... this was getting out of hand. First our mark turns out to be one of our top girls from within our *own* ranks, then she's got unexpected male *and* female company, and now it turns out there's a frickin' *pair* of Jacks, just to confuse things further.

"Hold on," I stood up as I turned towards the stairway brunette, who I noticed had strong blue highlights, and unmistakable piercings showing through the front of her blouse -- a club-scene regular, then --

one of our dealers, maybe, and a tall one ... probably played the role of a cougar. "I'm Jack, and you must be Anya?"

I extended my hand, and after a moment she grabbed it in a firm grasp. She had large hands, and was tall... and had a deep voice... and... an Adam's apple?

So maybe our mark... Denari, it must be... didn't actually have any female guests after all. Anya wasn't a clubbing *cougar* -- he was a *queen*.

S/he (?) took a look at the faces around the room, and seemed to see my surprise. "Why don't we all have a seat, Jack, and you can tell us what you're doing here." I could tell the Queen of Clubs (hey, it's how I think) was used to people listening to her. Looking at the reactions of Deena & Jack, she was definitely the leader of this group -- but for what, I still had no idea. She seemed to be a higher-up in the party-drug/club scene part of our organization. With Deena being one of us, and "Diamond" Jack, I suspected, being into the high-profit white collar endeavors -- this was definitely an unusual group after all. We generally keep to our own, and don't mix ranks well. Some games just don't allow for teamwork.

Deuce pulled over an end-table, and sat down. Deena took a chair, as did Anya... the other Jack stayed standing, beef stew abandoned at this point.

"Well," I began, searching for something to get them talking, and maybe get a clue as to what was going on, "I'm here on account of your *multi-jurisdictional* activities." They didn't know how much I knew, so I thought I'd play up my official role a bit.

"Well," Anya led, whether intentionally mimicking me or not I couldn't quite tell, "that's really none of your business, now is it?"

"You've got Denari involved, and so that *makes* it my business." I countered. "I have to protect our interests, both in our top girls like Deena, and in new endeavors that should be ours."

"Oh, I didn't get her involved..." she began.

"You're the leader of this trio" I cut her off, "you expect me to believe otherwise?"

"Hey, she was *assigned* to me, Mr. Lonely Hearts... which is something I'd have thought you would know." Anya stood up, "It's not as if I had much say in the matter, so you can just take it up with management directly."

I stood as well. "I guess I should, then." I just kept pushing through as if I knew where this was going... "I'll do it right now, I've got the authority to track this one all the way back."

She gave me a look I couldn't quite read.

"Be careful you don't stick your nose where it doesn't belong -- you mess this one up, and it'll take you down for good ... Jack." I looked at her coolly... did she know more about me than she was letting on?

"I know what I'm doing. Now get me in touch with the one who assigned Deena, or your little secret group's not going to be so secret anymore. How would management like that?"

"All right," she spread her hands "your funeral. You might as well go talk... Lakefront Alterra -- in the old river pumping station .. it's just about lunch time, that's where she'll be. I'd leave right away, just to be sure you don't miss her." I didn't like how I was being sent on my way... but I didn't really have any good reason to delay at this point, after what I'd just said.

"Well, it's been a *pleasure*..." I warily shook hands with Jack, and nodded to Deena, "I'll be seeing you again real soon, I'm sure."

I wasn't quite sure how Deuce and me and the three from the flophouse fit together yet... but there were definite possibilities, depending on who I was up against. I turned and headed out, assuming Deuce would follow. There was nothing further for me in here, without exposing how little I really knew about what was going on. And besides, I needed to get back before the meter ran out.

## Chapter 3
## The Bluff

"Jack-man, that was..." I looked back at Deuce as he came down the flophouse steps behind me, shaking his head, and I wondered how he'd finish that phrase. I wondered if my confusion had shown back there -- but something in front of us caught his attention instead. "Hey, Cassanova!" I turned back to the street to see two figures coming out of a silver Mitsubishi Spider parked across the street. The driving beat of techno was loud enough that I should have noticed when I came through the door, if I'd been paying proper attention. Trendy suits, but a bit rumpled. Both around 30, the one who had called out to me had an earring (silver, not a diamond), and looked pretty sure of himself. The other had two rings in an eyebrow, frosted tips on his spiky hair, and was walking a bit behind. Most likely these two were still finishing up last night at the clubs, and not just up early for a morning run to the bagel shop. I figured I was a match for the first guy if this went bad, but Spiky looked just as tough. Deuce would be almost useless, and I'd have to take them both on if it came to that.

"You know my name," I stopped on the sidewalk and half-turned away, making them come to meet us, but without the confrontation -- or implied respect --of facing them squarely (it's all about the posturing), "but I don't believe I remember you."

"That's because we haven't met." He made his bid to take the upper hand in the conversation, keeping his information close to his chest. "I didn't expect to see *you* at the meeting."

"Walk an' talk," I said as I started down the sidewalk towards the car, "I'm on a schedule." *And I've been at this game a lot longer than you have.*

"Hey!" He was forced to catch up, and Deuce & Spiky-hair fell in behind us as our group moved down the sidewalk -- away from the flophouse and towards their car. "What's the hurry, Cassanova? Grabbing a bagel before the meeting starts?" I'm not sure what the involvement of these two was, but the last thing I needed was another person trying to get in on this thing. The more players that got involved, the more chances that fate would pick someone else to smile on -- and there were already more people than I'd thought just a half hour ago.

"Before it starts?" I stopped and turned directly towards him, and it just happened we'd gotten almost even with his Mitsubishi. "Anya didn't tell you?" He knew who I was, but didn't know how I figured in, either...Anya's name definitely clicked with him, though. He seemed to be buying it so far, so I decided to go for the straight-up bluff, and see if I could get rid of him. "Wait a minute.. which one are you, anyway?"

"John."

"Well Johnny, we had to move up the schedule a bit, so I'd have time to get word back to the boss... we're already done. I stuck around to make the call, but the meeting broke up about 10 minutes ago and everybody else headed out." I leaned in a bit closer and shook my head. "You guys missed it."

"What about everybody else?"

"Well, Jack & Deena made it just fine?" Names have power. He pulled out his cell & checked it.

"I don't have any missed calls or messages or anything" he said, as he jumped right past suspicion and went straight to trying to defend himself. That gave me my angle. "Are we just meeting for the pickup tonight, then?" he asked, a bit worried, "I'd better call... uh... her."

"Ahhh..." I shook my head "... ok... if you think so..."

"What...?" He was holding the cell, but looking back and forth from Deuce to me. (C'mon, Deuce, play along!)

"Well..." I looked at Deuce, who just shrugged & looked away noncommittally (that was good enough, I can work with that), "*she* was pretty pissed. Said something about you partying all night, when there's more important things going on."

"Hey, nobody told me the time got changed!" He looked to Spiky for support "I didn't get the message! It's not my fault this time!" Spiky seemed pissed now, too, so Johnny held the phone out to show me. I reached out and tilted it away from the sun to take a better look... holding down the button for a moment to silence it. "When's the pickup?" he asked, "We gotta be there -- just in case."

"Yeah... that's the other thing, Johnny...since you weren't there... again..." I gestured to Deuce, "well I've got him along, and Jack said he'd just bring an extra guy too... apparently this is pretty much a small-team opportunity." I looked away, but then turned back to continue before he could respond, "Look, I don't know how else to say this... she doesn't want you there anymore."

"Dude," Deuce finally jumped in, "y'all might want to give her some space to calm down, if you know what I mean. Have you ever seen her really angry before?"

All right, it was time to wrap this up before one of the others actually came out of the house. "Tell you what," I offered, "I've got to call her back anyway -- I'll mentioned that you showed up, and tell her I saw her call didn't come through on your phone... and I'll have her call you if she changes her mind and wants you two there." I looked him straight in the eyes, "that's the best I can do at this point, John."

"Jack," Deuce looked at his watch, "we really gotta be goin' or we'll miss the next meeting, and be in da same mess John be in."

"You're right, we'd all better get out of here." I looked pointedly at Johnny -- "and turn the music down, you've probably attracted attention." That got him into his car, and Spiky took the cue to go around to his side as well. "Good luck!" I said as I turned and walked off. Before we'd gone half the block, I head the Spider drive away. They'd bought our bluff, and hopefully were out for the rest of the affair -- and I was beginning to get a better idea of how we could play this out.

Four minutes still on the meter, I noticed as I walked up, got in and started up the car. I rolled down the window *and* turned on the air -- I needed to cool down after that. Once he'd closed his door, Deuce just turned and looked at me, with his arms crossed and head tilted a bit, and waited.

"Deuce... look-"

"What are you gettin' me into, Jack?" (he'd been waiting to cut me off, apparently). "They're gonna find out what you just did. What *we* just did." his eyes widened at the realization, and he turned & looked out the window. "I don't think I want any more to do with this one -- you gettin' reckless."

"Deuce, they'll back me if it looks like I've got the winning story -- you know they will."

"An they'll just as quickly join whoever else seems like they're going to come out on top... they're neutral, with no loyalty to you." He reached for the door handle, "me, I'm not neutral. I got enough loyalty to you to leave before I end up being used against you, Jack." He got out. "Good luck."

I watched him walk away, and wondered if that would have been the smart thing to do.

* * *

"You lovers get in an argument and he walked out on you, pretty boy?"

*Now what?* I turned to see a black Jaguar convertible -- top down -- pulled up beside me, neatly blocking my ability to pull out from my parking spot. Two people inside. The speaker from the passenger seat had very red lipstick outlining a mocking smile... and large diamond earrings, which somehow matched the predatory glint in eyes like ice. These two weren't even trying to be subtle -- they wanted people to know who they were.

"Get in." Commanded the driver. I wasn't *sure* who he was, but he seemed like he was used to being listened to. The woman opened the door and got out, then held it open for me.

"You sit in front," she purred, and patted the leather. "I'll be right behind you." Her voice, her words, her mouth were all flirtatious -- but that playfulness never touched her diamond-cold eyes. I glared at her, and shut off the engine. I could tell this wasn't one of those requests that I had the option of turning down. Just to assert a small measure of independence, I grabbed a handful of change. I got out of the car, looked at them both, and then walked around the front of the car to the meter. I plugged in two dollars worth of quarters. That gave me two more hours. With that, I walked back and got into the Jag, with the ice queen and her king.

"What's this all about?" I asked, fishing for some hint of what I was in for with these two.

"We just want to have a little chat..." she said from the backseat, "about that meeting you just attended."

"And maybe give you a word of warning," the driver added, without so much as glancing in my direction as he put the Jag in gear and began to drive.

"I hope this doesn't take too long," I said, "I was on my way to meet someone for lunch."

"No problem!" she said, "we'll take you there, and we can chat on the way," -- as if this really was just a friendly discussion. "Where to?" They were feeling me out, trying to learn what they could about how strong a position I was in. I decided to continue trying to ride the bluff that had worked on Johnny.

"Head towards the Lakefront." Better not to give them much detail. "Why does my business concern you? Are there matters of the heart you two need help with?"

"Oh, it's *your* business, is it?" the driver asked. "You sure about that? We were thinking this was *our* business, and you were just some idiot who was about to overstep his limits trying to look like he could play with the big boys." OK, so he wasn't the subtle type. "I'm surprised you to even got as far as seeing Anya, Jack & the others at the flophouse."

"Hmmm..." I paused. Apparently he thought he was in a strong enough position to ignore my bluff entirely, "well, I'm not at all surprised that you're confused. I guess we'll have to just see how it all plays out tonight."

"Listen, *Jack*," he turned his head and looked at me for the first time... I must have struck a nerve, "after tonight, I'm going to take over this operation -- and I don't recall planning on having you be a part of it. In fact, from what I'd heard from Anya, even under the present leadership, you were specifically *out* of this one." Now *that* was an interesting bit of information.

"Things change," I said, and mentally added *on the fly sometimes.* From what he just said, Anya would certainly pair up with him and the Ice Queen before Deuce and me, and this guy knew it. I needed him a little less sure of his position. "I'm on my way to check in with the 'present leadership' right now, and I'll be sure to ask what they think about your side planning."

"Anya didn't say..." he looked skeptical.

"Arthur," she interrupted from the back seat, "you know, *we* haven't had lunch yet either." She leaned forward to be closer to my ear, "you wouldn't mind if we joined you -- would you, Jack?" She leaned back, "in fact, lunch is on us. I insist."

Chapter 4
**A Strange Turn**

We pulled slowly into the Alterra parking lot, which was always full around lunch time. As a student with their backpack & coffee walked in front of the Jag, I said "I'll see you inside," and suddenly opened the door and got out. I shut the door behind me before the Ice Queen could get out from the back seat, and headed inside. They knew I wasn't going anywhere else while they parked, so I figured I'd have maybe 3-5 minutes before they came in.

I scanned the tables on the lowest level of the greatroom. Anya had unhelpfully just said it was a "her," but I was assuming I'd be able to spot someone from the organization... nope. One guy sitting alone, that could maybe be involved... except that as I approached him, I noticed he was still wearing his Starbucks name badge. A quick look in the adjacent pump-room yielded nothing, either, so I headed up the open stairway to the upper level, scanning faces as I went.

*Oh my god.* It couldn't be -- fate would not be that cruel to me at this point. I took one more look around, and decided that *her* being here couldn't possibly be coincidence. Anya's attitude about this meeting made much more sense, now. I tried to wrap my head around this bizarre turn of events. Taking a deep breath, I headed for the table. I didn't have much time before the other players in this game joined us.

She was a sitting alone at a two-person table in the corner, talking on her mobile, and the opposite chair uninvitingly held her bag. I walked up and moved it. "Mind if I sit down?"

"I'll have to call you back," she said flatly into the phone, and then snapped it shut. "What the hell are *you* doing here? Didn't I give you enough to work on with the issues at the Maple street operation last night?" I sat down anyway, across from the heartless witch that was the closest thing I had to a boss.

She was an older woman, with vivid red hair, and I'd heard her described as "stately" before -- but she still tried too hard to look like one of the girls at the houses she ran, and the result wasn't a good one. However, her word was law in the bordellos, and on anything pertaining to the escorts or dancers & their activities -- the 'Queen of Hearts,' as I liked to think of her, as deranged as the one from Alice -- but she'd never managed to actually move any higher in the organization. She seemed to believe it was because she started out as 'merchandise,' and the bosses could never quite see beyond that. And she was bitter about that fact.

I'd rubbed her the wrong way from the start, and as far as I could tell she'd been actively working to get me out of the organization ever since. There was no love lost between the Queen of Hearts and I.

"Look, there's a problem, and there's not much time to discuss it," I started.

"Why should I care about *your* problems over *my* lunch break?" She said too loudly. Her lips were pressed together, and her eyes fierce.

I leaned forward across the table, "They're about to become your problems. They'll be walking up the stairs in about 30 seconds, and they're going to try to take over after the pickup tonight, unless we at least pretend to be a unified front!"

She looked back at the stairway, "what are you talking about?"

"Look, Madge, I met with Anya, Jack & Denari this morning, and Deuce & I've already replaced Johnny and his friend for the pick-up tonight." Let's see how she reacts to that.

"You," she shook her head slowly as she looked at me, "have no idea what you're talking about, do you? You idiot, if you've messed this up...."

"I don't know what kind of side play you had going on here, but this should fall under *our* business -- and these two coming up the stairs" I gestured towards them as I leaned back, and tried to look relaxed, "plan to co-opt the operation for their own at the first opportunity."

She leaned back, and crossed her legs, and flashed me an evil, self-satisfied smile. "What makes you think I wouldn't want to go along with that plan?" she countered.
*Uh oh.*

## Chapter 5
### All in

She stood as the two approached the table, and extended her hand to them. "Jack told me you'd be joining us, but I'm afraid all the bigger tables are taken -- you'll have to pull up some chairs." Arthur grabbed two chairs, as his partner shook Madge's hand.

"I'm Iris, and this is Arthur." -- the Ice Queen's flirty purr was gone, replaced by a crisp and efficient alto.

"Madge." my boss replied coolly, "Apparently you wanted to meet *before* tonight's events?"

"We've got a proposal I think you'll be interested in" Arthur leaned in as he spoke, "but it might change a bit how things go down tonight at the river."

"I'm listening." Madge wasn't volunteering much, but wasn't shutting him down either.

"Well, this thing could really best be handled by someone with the proper resources... resources you frankly don't have at the moment. Especially with everything else you've got going on, you already know you're likely to get this taken away & given to someone else." Arthur gestured to include himself and Iris, "We could give you the resources you'd need, to manage this operation on our behalf -- *if* you can manipulate events at the warehouse to ensure that it ends up in our hands."

"Why not just take it direct from the courier?" she questioned, "why do you need me at all?"

"Because," Iris jumped in, "until they show up at 8, we don't have any more idea who that is than you do. And we don't know how the talks went among the bosses, or who came out on top...this might not be something we can take over quite so blatantly on our own." She eased back in her chair, and looked around the room... I was almost surprised by how blatantly these two were playing Madge, as Iris let out a little line, before Arthur leaned in to set the hook.

"Look," he said, "We know it will be a small team that launches this thing -- probably not more than five initially. But we won't know what the right mix is until we're there, and we want to go in with the heaviest hitters we can." *Here it comes...* "that's why we want you."

This was not going at all the way I needed it to -- and so far I wasn't even part of the conversation. "Look Madge," I said, "you're not really buying this, are you?"

"Why shouldn't I, Jack?"

"Yes, why shouldn't she want to be part of the stronger team?" Arthur asked, "And for that matter, I'm surprised you're not trying to join up." he looked to Iris, "I'm sure we could find something for him to do...?"

This was it, this was the moment. I really couldn't make a higher offer here, so it was all or nothing. I could give in to these two -- and if they were successful, maybe continue working for them. Actually, it was now looking like, continue working for Madge, except she'd be getting her orders from them.

Or, I could take my chances on my own... and if they came out on top tonight, I'd be done. Madge would be sure to see me conveniently gotten rid of, for knowing how she'd helped them. But if they didn't win.. they might take Madge down with them.

I couldn't keep going like I had been, just treading water and hoping not to get taken out by one of the sharks. I had to go for it. "Delightful as that sounds," I answered, "I think I'll have to decline -- and you should, too, Madge."

"You and Deuce," Madge asked incredulously, "you think I'd take your advice over *Arthur Koning's*?"

Well, that confirmed it. I knew that last name, and that meant these two were just who I thought they were. Iris was about equal with Madge and Anya in the organization.. if *both* sided with her, I couldn't see anything coming up that could help me beat the three of them. Not only that, but Arthur Koning was plugged in to the highest level of the organization, one level below the bosses themselves. If one of the other "Kings" showed up tonight, the two of them and the three queens would shut me out easily. For that matter, if a boss showed up, he'd be sure to have their backing, as well -- and with a number-one, first level boss, King Arthur, Iris the Ice Queen, Diamond Jack, and our "10" girl Denari -- he wouldn't even need Anya or Madge -- he'd have a complete line-up to take this thing forward.

"Maybe, Jack" Arthur leaned in towards me "you'd better not come after all. Doesn't seem likely to be a very smart play for you. Drop out while you still can keep your head above water."

My head was spinning. There were just too many ways that they could come out on top. Maybe if the courier turned out to be another "Jack" that showed tonight -- someone in the middle ranks like me, looking for the win that would cement them in the upper circles -- I could convince them & Diamond that our interests were best served together, instead of under the rule of Arthur & Iris.. and then Madge & Anya would have to side with the three of us. A full boat like that could keep me from drowning here... maybe I could still pull this thing out...

"Oh, I'll be there." I countered, "and we'll see who comes out on top."

Well, that was it. I was all in -- and the odds didn't look too good from here.

## Chapter 6
### Down by the River

After that, there hadn't been much more to say.  Koning left (didn't give me a ride back to my car, of course), and I wasn't going to spend what could be my last free afternoon any closer to Madge than I had to.  I called Deuce to come pick me up... but he didn't answer.  Probably still upset with me from earlier. I ended up taking a cab back to my car.  Made it with time to spare on the meter.

By 7:30 that night, I still hadn't heard from Deuce, even after a couple more calls.  I'd really been hoping I could convince him to back me up tonight... even tried filling him in about Madge secretly siding with Koning, and me needing him if we were going to keep this within our team -- in case he was listening to his machine on the other end. I guess, though, he'd meant what he said earlier. And I couldn't really blame him... though I did anyway.

I was parked a couple blocks from the River, at the place I was certain they'd been talking about at lunch.  I'd been trying hard to seem like I already knew everything, so they'd be open with information, and I hadn't exactly confirmed the location with anyone.  Luckily there was only one place the organization had a stake in that matched.  From where I was, I could see down the road to the parking entrance on the opposite side of the street from me.  The place had seemed empty when I came by, and I hadn't seen anyone go in or out in the half-hour I'd been here watching.

Until now.

A car had just gone in, pausing by the door while it automatically opened, and giving me time to discreetly (I hoped) use my mini binoculars to see who the driver was. Luckily it was a hot night, and Madge had her windows open. As the overhead door rolled down behind her, I wondered what would happen if I got up there, and it just didn't open for me. Wouldn't exactly make the best impression of my relevance in this thing. On the other hand, it wasn't like I could sneak in... I'd made it clear who I was and why I was going to be here... no use trying to be secretive at this point. I was playing this thing exposed, and it all came down to what happened once I stepped inside that building.

After a moment's deliberation, I decided to walk up & try to use the personnel door. If they didn't want to let me in, I could always... well, I was sure I'd come up with something. About a block away, I heard a car turn down the side-street the warehouse was on. There wasn't much else down here, and the road ended at the river, so there was a good bet this was another one coming to the party. As it neared me and slowed down, I turned, expecting to see Koning's Jag. Instead, it was an Audi, and Anya was at the wheel.

"Jack," she called, "hop in, I'll give you a lift."

It seemed a little silly, this close to the door, but at least this way I'd be sure to get inside the building. I walked around the car and got in, expecting to see the other two from the morning -- but the car was empty.

"Thanks," I said... "Why?"

"I wanted to talk to you before we got inside, Jack. I heard about what you did... I think it's all in the open at this point." She looked down for a moment, then back at me, "Loyalty to one's own part of the organization is *so* last season. Though it is nice to imagine things still work that way sometimes." She squirmed a little in her seat, and I saw the corners of her mouth pull downward just a bit, "I have to admit, I'm not crazy about working with Koning. But I will. The same goes for Jack... and even Denari -- though I know she would rather be working with you. If somehow you pull off a miracle in there, and come out on top, we'll work with you. But if things are going his way after the courier arrives and all the cards are on the table, well... you know who's team we're on." She eased the car the rest of the way down the street, and looked straight ahead while she waited for the door to go up. "I'm sorry, but that's the way it is, and I thought you should know."

We pulled inside, and the door closed behind us. Mostly empty warehouse space, there were a few other cars present, parked off to one side. Light was still coming in the dirty windows. It lent a gloomy atmosphere as dusk approached outside -- but no one had yet moved to turn on any of the artificial lights. Instead, Denari, Jack and Madge were standing together talking, with Jack leaning up against Madge's car. They looked comfortable enough with each other... and didn't seem too concerned about how this would all play out. I guess they didn't have as much to gain -- or especially to lose -- in this whole thing.

Could I put together a winning team out of this group?

We got out, and started walking over towards the others. Just then the door opened again, and Koning pulled in, with Iris in the seat at his side. He pulled up aggressively, cutting me off and stopping abruptly next to where I was standing, and killed the engine.

Opening his door, he stepped out, looking at me across the soft-top. "So, Jack... you decided to come to my party after all. Not a good play."

"We'll see, Koning." I hoped I sounded more certain than I felt. I glanced down at my watch -- almost eight. I really wished I'd gotten a hold of Deuce... it was always easier to play things cool when I was "demonstrating" for his benefit. The kid had a lot to learn... but I guess, in all honesty, I had to admit that I was a lot more comfortable when I knew the rookie had my back. And he had a solid ear to the beat of the street... he'd be a good asset, if I hadn't driven him away.

"Jack, dear" Iris drawled as I stepped quickly aside from the door she opened into where I had just been standing, "it's not too late to hide in our trunk and pretend you aren't here." She stepped out and gestured invitingly.

I didn't bother to respond to her baiting. It wouldn't help me in front of the others at this point, and I was too nervous to think of anything good to say anyway.

The door rolled up one more time, and a dark sedan pulled in. It was impossible to see who was inside, with the tinted windows and the increasing gloom inside the warehouse. As the sedan cut its engine, there was a moment of stillness as everyone waited, and the waves of the river could be heard lapping against the walls outside.

The overhead door rolled down, covering the water's noise, but still no one moved. Someone's watch softly chimed. *Eight o'clock.*

The automated lights kicked on, as afternoon officially gave way to evening. Someone got out of the sedan, and walked around to open the passenger's door. I squinted, my eyes still adjusting to the sudden brightness of the overhead lights... was that... Deuce?

He held the door as someone handed him something and stepped out -- someone that I didn't recognize. As the figure approached, a few things became apparent about him. He was an older gentleman, and used a cane, though it almost seemed more an accessory to his suit than a physical necessity. Grey hair, good looks, probably in his mid 60s? He was smiling broadly as he approached, and it was then that I noticed the look of shock on Madge's face. "sir..." she murmured weakly...

"Thank you all for coming out to welcome me here tonight!" His quiet, animated voice took control of the room instantly. "Nice to see you again, Madge... and you, Arthur." Koning didn't say a word.

"Sir," Madge said, " I wasn't expecting you, or any of the highest level. I thought we were just meeting a courier, sir."

"I know what you thought, Madge." he gave her a sharp look. "I know all about the rumors and plotting, and the politics going on around this project. That's why the other bosses and I decided I'd keep a personal involvement in this affair."

That was it then. This was one of the top four, and Koning would have a straight, unbroken connection from the highest level down to Denari's presence on the street. So much for Koning's needing Madge...

"Sir," she said again, more strongly this time, "with all that you've got going on, you're sure to need someone here who can be more directly involved in managing things on your behalf..." she must realize Koning's position... what was she going after? "I think I've got a demonstrated record of managing things effectively for you in the past." *For you...?* Wait, was this ...'our' boss? I'd never met him, and frankly for some reason it hadn't occurred to me that this could be

"Ace" Corazon himself, another one of us... but then Deuce showing up as his driver made a lot more sense. "I'd be honored to continue filling that roll for you, Mr. Corazon."

That was definitely him. I didn't even know the last time he had come to the States, and I had never had a chance to interact with him directly like Madge occasionally did. "I know, Madge, I know," he looked directly into her eyes, "but I still need you doing those very things you refer to. You may well be involved in this new venture, but someone else will be taking point on this one." He turned to face Arthur & me.

Iris laughed, "Sorry Madge... it was a nice try, but Arthur's far more experienced at these things."

"Actually, Miss" said Corazon, "I'm thinking this new launch will require a close-knit team, able to work tightly together. Deuce here has been sharing his thoughts on the organizational dynamics here in Milwaukee, and especially on how things have played out today. I think I've decided we might have the best chances of success if we kept with an established team on this one, following a leader who's a bit more flexible, and willing to take a chance or two. Our situations can't always be under our control -- but it's how we react to them that determines if our outcomes are successful."

Koning's lips tightened, and he gave me a look I didn't quite understand. I looked back to find everyone looking at me... Anya, Jack, Denari, Iris, Madge... even Corazon. It slowly dawned on me. With our Boss at the head of this venture, wanting to keep to an established team, that meant he wasn't looking to use the more straight team Koning had proposed after all...

And the only team here stronger even than Koning's, then was us "Hearts." And if Madge wasn't in charge, then that left... me? Deuce walked up and handed me the case he'd been holding. "I tol' im I been followin you even against my better judgement for months now... just can't seem to help it." He shook his head, "he must'a thought I meant dhat in a good way." He grinned as he stepped back.

Corazon held out his hand to me. "Good to finally meet you, Jack. Get the rest of our team together and let's go somewhere more suitable. You pick the place, and tell the rest of our team, but I want you to ride with me." He turned and headed back towards the sedan.

"As for the rest of you, thanks for coming out to welcome me. I'm sure we'll be in touch over the next week while I'm in town." He turned back towards the group, and with a frosty edge on his voice for the first time. "And I'd like to say right now how grateful I am for all the support I'm sure you'll give Jack on this project going forward." He continued on into the sedan.

      "Where we going, Jack?" asked Madge, far more pleasantly than expected, as she walked up to me. She must have seen my surprise at her tone. "Oh, don't be like that, Jack..." she looked back at Koning and Iris, "Denari and I will follow you. We *are* on the same team, after all."

      Well, that was it. It had paid off. Just like that, I was suddenly back on top. Corazon, Madge, Denari, Deuce & I were heading off to orchestrate the biggest new venture our organization had seen in years -- and I was running the show. The tip Deuce had given me had started this whole thing off just a day ago, and it looked like whatever he told Corazon about me had really helped make this possible.

      "No card can help you..." but I guess when you're out of options, with a good bluff even a Deuce in the right place can make a winning hand.

## No Card Can Help You

A student of martial arts, a multi-sport enthusiast, and an aspiring author, **Andrew Allen** has realized that you don't have to be good at your hobbies to enjoy them immensely. He has two incredible daughters who love to read, and the greatest fiancee within 6,260 miles.

# Poke Her

*Matthew J. Kolell*

## *Poke Her*

"Poker!?!? I don't even know her!!" roars Balthazar, as Roberto's chick sits down at the table.

Fernando replies, "That's the only way any one would want to poke her. As soon as you get to know her, you don't want to even touch her."

Balthazar continues to roar with laughter as he slaps her thigh saying, "you gonna let him talk about you like that?"

"Come on, lets play, she's got money to give us. I saw her with four or five guys before I came in. Or was it more?" states Fernando.

"Hey baby, how much did you get from Fernando before he got to 'know you'?" jibes Balthazar.

"Eff off Balt, the only part of me that has touched her is the back of my hand. Are you gonna deal or what, Ali?"

"I'll deal as soon as she gets some money out, and I guess you don't count it as touching her if you have protection?" replies Alejandro.

Balthazar places his large hand on her thigh, "Hey babe, how come I'm the only one here who hasn't had to pay?" Laughing again, "You have your money up here?" as he slides his hand under her skirt.

Pulling a roll of money out of her purse, she deftly brushes aside Balt's hand as she lays the money on the table.

Ali deals the cards to the five of them while Roberto pushes the chips to her. As she calls, Fernando blurts out, "Hopefully it's as easy to get her money as it is to get with her."

"Fernando! Lighten up, how long were you waiting to use that line?" Ali responds while folding his 4, 7 offsuit.

"I call. At least she's making money with her looks because she can't rely on her brains," says Fernando.

"Not everyone's as lucky as I am to have both of those," Balt chortles while rapping his knuckles to check. "Not even you guys can match me in either category."

♥♥♥♥♥

Her blond hair waved softly in the wind as she looked out over the city from her roof. The sun cast a red shadow over the city as it set, or was that just the blood that stained the fractured walls of the buildings. She used to love being there; it was her sanctuary from her father and friends and expectations. Now she longed for that once again: to feel safe, to have a place of her own, but have friends and family to go back to. The city and fading light only reminded her of what had been lost; the walls were crumbling before her and she knew the black of night would soon envelop her.

Her brains and beauty made the other girls in the village jealous of her, but her style and status still won her friends. She was quick witted, although her education was lacking in the skills she had needed to survive when the killing came. Still, she had her sex appeal; men would pray for a gust of wind just to get a peak at her tanned thighs as her skirt would rise as she walked past. It wasn't just her body, it was who she was that made men want to love her, use her, be seen with her or even just talk to her. That was the constant, before, during and even when, or if, the fighting would end.

She decided to try in the morning. She had never been up there at that time of day. Maybe the rising sun would give back her sanctuary.

♥♥♥♥♥

"Ha! Two heart flushes but her king beats your seven, Fernando," chuckles Balthazar.

"I thought the seven would be lucky but when you get lucky as much as she does, you can't compete with that," sighs Fernando.

"Need a massage to release some of those nerves?" Balthazar cups her breast in his massive paw. "Maybe some of that luck will rub off on me now. Hey, at least you win the deal, Fernan."

♣♣♣♣♣

Balthazar was our ticket. He ranked high enough to get us in anywhere he pleased. Most of the insurgents had finished being chased from the city and a modicum of normality had been restored. "Lets get out of this hole and see where the upper crust go to have a good time," Balt ordered. We'd get free booze and food and out of our dump for a barracks. But that ass had to choose that night and that club of all the places to go. In his defense there weren't many places.

As soon as I laid eyes on her, I hated her. She wouldn't choose me over the others. I didn't have the face nor social skills of Roberto or Alejandro. And I didn't have the power nor rank of Balthazar. I was bigger than any of them but she wouldn't know that, not like I'd want her to anyway.

She sat at the bar in her black dress, with her high heel dangling from her foot. She still had to give the guys something to look at even though her father had died some days earlier. THEN those assholes tell me they know her. That this is their hometown. Nine effing months in the same unit with those two, eating, sleeping and killing alongside them. Been in the city for three weeks and they don't mention it until now. I just thought they were next in line for promotions when they had their strategy meetings before entering the city.

Roberto says this is his ticket. She'll need him for protection and he needs her as a cover; besides she'll have money stashed somewhere for after the war. But what about me you ass, I'm the one running from my past. Some even suspect me here, and you'll get found out too. Then I notice Ali staring daggers as Berto strolls over to her.

"She has a bigger pair than yours, Fernan," says Balt.

"She'd be lucky to have a pair as big as mine, though it would

cut down on her business when she laughs at all the other guys,"
Fernando replies.

"Why? Because she'd be reminded of how you couldn't get it
up," Alejandro chimes in.

"Ali, I don't know how any guy could get it up for her with
everyone she's been with," snaps Fernando.

"I've already dealt, lets play.  And besides, with all the money
we're giving her, she'll be just fine, won't you babe?" Balt places his
hand softly under her chin to raise her head towards his.  "You know
I'm just having some fun."

♠♠♠♠♠

"I do," answered Roberto.

The church dwarfed the small gathering.  It had survived
mostly unmarred except for a few stray bullets.  The only building in
town that managed to stay unmolested even if its people weren't. The
empty pews spread out behind the couple, while a scarlet glow spread
over them through the stained glass as night began to set in.

As they turned to walk down the aisle together, the priest
caught Roberto's arm. "There is the matter of payment yet."

"I believe my friend and I settled the debt last night old man,"
Roberto hissed.

The distraction gave Alejandro enough time to slip through the huge doors unnoticed.  The bride was too busy looking down to notice.

♠♠♠♠♠

"HA! She won again!" Balt shouts as he lays the final card down.

"Punk ass river rat!" rants Fernando.  "She sucked out again."

"I here your the one that likes to suck out, at least according to Roberto," says Ali.

Balthazar slides over and pulls her up onto his lap. "So where are we going tonight to celebrate?  Maybe we can suck some face."

"Can't go back to your place because you won't have any money left either at the rate she's going," Fernan states.

"Balt, put her down," Ali says. "She has to deal."

♦♦♦♦♦

A sick feeling settled into the pit of his stomach as they marched over the hill.  There she was, silhouetted in the setting sun.  Her body shimmering as the heat left the city beneath her.

## Poke Her

She had taken him there once and the next day he left. War was coming. It was inevitable. It was stay and fight and die. Join the impotent army and be separated forever. Or join the army that would win. It made sense; it was his best chance at survival. Their best chance for survival, for a possible life together. But he knew he was simply running away.

He recalled how he felt when he ran from her house. What if she told her friends? Or worse, his friends or family. She was so beautiful, standing there with the sun behind her outlining her perfect figure with her robe down at her feet. He couldn't control it, isn't that how nature works.

He tried to make her understand why he had to leave. It's hard when you can't even persuade yourself.

◆◆◆◆◆

"Agh! Straight!" shreiks Fernando.

"You went all in on a pair! That's hilarious," Balthazar laughs.

"She got an effing straight. She got something straight last night, right up her..," sneers Fernando.

"Who are you to talk about straight?" interrupts Alejandro.

Balthazar talking over Ali, "Speaking of last night, what were you two doing in there, Fernan."

"Roberto! She's your wife. Are you going to stand up for her at all?" challenges Alejandro.

"If I didn't know any better," Balthazar continues on. "...What!?... They're married!? When did this happen?"

"Screw you Ali. Grab your money and lets go, babe," Roberto shouts as he storms to the door.

"Where are you going, its your deal, Berto?" Balt calls after him. "Whats going on here?"

"Its a shame. A city sits there on the border. Two different cultures find out how to live together, work together, play together.. hell even sleep with each other. They become friends and respect each other and their differences. Then one country wants something they have or is pissed at the other and they're caught in the middle."

"Balt, if you think about this too hard you'll wind up giving yourself a headache or worse, you'll blow your brains out. What we do is awful, but this is war. At least its respectable, we let them know we're coming and taking over. They infiltrate our cities and blow up our buildings, killing men, women and children, while they hide in churches, schools and hospitals and expect our army to spare them."

"You're right general. Look at those two over there. He's from here. Her father just died and maybe those two can find and comfort each other; which might not have happened if it weren't for this war. They could have just gone along living in the same city, passing each other by and never find love. I would have gone over there myself and broken them up, if they didn't look so good together."

"They might look pretty together, but keep an eye on them Balt. He knows where to get his 'love.' Nothing good can come of it."

"Yes, sir."

An explosion booms outside the building, propelling Roberto back in, striking his wife and the table. Balthazar, Alejandro and Fernando are on their feet with guns out before Roberto drops dead. She crumples from the chair as her blood flows across her face, pooling on the floor.

The blood is the same color as her lips. Those lips he kissed. The lips he softly touched. And the lips that he would just watch as they talked together. She had captivated him and still did. He knew he could love her and be the man that, as of yet, he had failed to be. If only she was still... Alejandro asks, "Is she still breathing?"

Balthazar replies, "I don't know. Poke her."

*Matthew J. Kolell*

44

**Matthew Kolell** *is not a best-selling author nor an award winning novelist. He does own a small business and enjoys gaming, bicycling, drinking Mountain Dew and spending time with his family. He lives in the Fox River Valley with his wife Sara, three sons, a beautiful daughter, a tall dining room table and their dog Ajax, a Great Dane mix.*

# Last Man Dying

*Catalino Tolejano, II*

## I.

I shall be immortal.

Those four words have defined what many would call a stellar legacy of military perfection.

Ever since I was a stubborn and defiant child I've lived a life of privilege and fear. Fear I was never going to measure up to my father and his fathers. Fear I was never going to be the man my mother wanted me to be, simply because if I were able to make my father proud I knew my mother would be disappointed. Privileged. I come from a long line of heroes, men who traced their forefathers through history as members of nearly every pivotal military conflict in their lifetimes, through generations of recorded human history.

I shall be immortal.

I've made my life a crusade toward the fulfillment of those words. With 12 of the top 15 NAF(North American Federation) Air Force awards, including what is still called the CMH. It's ironic, that at the celebration following my NMH(NAF Medal of Honor) ceremony, my mother gushed about how proud she was at the man I'd grown into - yet I could still see the pain and heartbreak behind her loving facade. She always felt I'd missed out on life's true accomplishments by never having a family, and never really spending time with what family I did have. One of my greatest moments of immortality, fire-linked to the bottomless guilt of a child whose achievements and fame only stir more sorrow in the eyes of his mother.

That was the last ceremony she'd attended.

Blast it! Well, at least I'd lasted about 80 relative minutes before the Curse hit. Sit in a carrier for months and never stumble down memory lane. Sit in a fighter's Core and everyone gets the Curse. Better probably to dwell on the past rather than the Curse. Damned psychologists. Or is it psychiatrists? In either case, no one ever noticed nor mentioned an issue until they had to psychoanalyze the minds of the new age of pilots. Science.<mental scoff> Where was I?

I keyed in the activation code for Gorgon Flight to deploy on station for our run, then repeated the sequence with Minotaur Flight's similar command codes and felt like the iconic monkey - just there to hit buttons at this point!

I suppose the nicest thing about commanding a squadron is, beside the joys of OSC (On-Site Command) responsibility, would be the right to name your Flights and configurations based on your own choosing, provided you don't break any regs, give up mission information, nor choose monikers that are obscene or forbidden. The big-nuts gave out the high-level squadron designation, Azure Squadron in my case, but all 60 of us squadron commanders got to name our own Flights. Half the squadron commanders used the manual's suggestions - older Country names, former wartime commanders, generals, colors or numbers. About two thirds of the rest went with Star Wars references. Seriously. The Vid is 100 years old and still the go-to reference for anyone crazy enough to come out here. And I mean the originals, not the redux trilogy around the 2040s. Then there's always us eclectic types to make up the rest. Carter had Skull, Vermillion, Invid, and Kyron – not sure I get that one even after he tried to explain it, once. Nguyen has Avengers, JLA, Grendel, and Lobo Flights. And yours truly takes home dual honors as the oldest guy in a fighter's Core and the oldest (so I'm told!) reference set of Flight call-signs: Cerberus, Gorgon, Minotaur, and Kraken usually.

Greek Mythology always made me think about whether the characters in those tales knew they were living history? It's hard to see it in the moment it's there. And often, once you've figured out that you're making history, the moment is seven clicks behind you and you didn't even say anything witty.

I shall be immortal.

Three days after mother passed, which feels like a lifetime ago, the world was made aware of our first true discovery of extraterrestrial life. But rather than the anticipation or elation you may expect, there was instead a collective sense of foreboding and fear. We KNEW they were there, and they were coming to us.

The beginning never seems like the beginning when you're living it. History gives us a perspective of the people, the sights, the sounds, the smells of the turning points in the course of human history. People talk about the way their small worlds skewed during these tumultuous events. None of it does justice to the acrid, looming presence of fundamental change weighing down on the heart of the world. All hell broke loose. Rioting. Murder. Political coups. Open war like we've never seen, scouring the Earth like a plague, and all developing at the same time across the Globe. Religious fervor spiked to unprecedented levels. Religions became the richest entities on the planet as money poured in to save souls.

It was pandemonium.

It was 6 months that saw about 2.4 billion souls lost through outright violence, suicide, and religious sacrifice.

It was 6 months that showed us the darkest sides of humanity.

It was 6 months that showed us what happens when nearly 200 countries across the globe panic and tear not only themselves but their friends and neighbors apart.

It was 6 months that led to the most terrible and amazing 9 months in human history. In June of 2058, almost all the leaders of the planet agreed on a whole new Free Earth Federation based on a loosely democratic society consisting of the 7 major 'traditional' geographic areas of the world. In those 9 months, accords were made across the globe giving birth to a new world like nothing you'd have thought possible in the years before.

It was a new order of freedom, camaraderie, social consciousness, and acceptance the likes of which and a scale of which humans had never achieved!

Unless you were one of the countries that didn't sign on. In just 3 months 11 countries ceased, in essence, to exist. They had no import nor export, no friends really, and only 183 or so unified foes. 6 were overrun outright in the beginning, as if they were petulant children who just needed to be disciplined for their disobedience.

The other 5 held on until their people destroyed their governments themselves. National pride only goes so far when you can't get food nor water brought into a desert. People will fight change until their families starve and their neighbors are dying. It's an awful legacy for peace, but a necessary lesson that only strengthened the FEF when the last 'renegade' nations were brought into the arms of our enlightenment.

I shall be immortal.

Would the Greek Gods have fared any better? Will I be remembered as Hermes or Achilles?

## II.

*<Alpha Echo 13, confirm "Go" status and position,>* came word from the carrier, the Canada.

"Canada, this is Alpha Echo 13. Azure squadron deployed and on station at 6 light seconds, position Yankee 3."

It's funny how the mind can wander. I've been sitting here in my command fighter for about 40 relative minutes waiting for an operational authorization. Eighty minutes were spent in transit to Yankee 3. As humans meet 'face-to-face' with an extrasolar species for the first time, I've spent two relative hours LEAVING the most historic event in human history. Because, as fate would have it, I draw the furthest assignment: Deep Patrol or DP. And I got scrambled early out of the biggest poker pot of the trip so I could sit out here and patrol for OTHER extrasolar species! Or maybe the imaginary band of Earth-rejects building their magical rebel fleet out at Ceres? Unfortunately the most I have to look forward to is a nap or the remote chance to intercept some space debris headed anywhere near the meeting site!

*<Alpha Echo 13, confirmed. Proceed on mission. Sorry to leave you out in the sticks, Ortiz. Just your crappy luck-of-the-draw piling on to the misery waiting for you here when you get back! Poor bastard. Canada out.>*

Major Paulsen really did have a way with words. As XO of the Canada, she had the latitude to hassle anyone she wanted, really, at any time. She and I go back almost 30 years crossing paths. She's a brilliant tactician and thinks on her feet faster than anyone I've ever even heard of. Of course, that means her mouth sometimes operates ahead of her common sense, hence she's just the XO. Not like she's insubordinate, she's just smart, knows it, and (unfortunately for her) is usually right. Brass doesn't take well to someone that good calling their mistakes, even unintentionally. Compounding this would be the fact that she's a knockout at 50 and probably doesn't know that her various pictures from staff shoots and press conferences adorn better than half the engineering crew lockers. Nothing sexier to an engineer than a commanding officer who gets her hands dirty and looks good doing it.

"Roger Canada, Commencing patrol. Next audcomm in 92 minutes, relative. Mark. Your two pair aren't going to cut it this time, Major. I recommend you go down there and fold now before you get caught up in a fire drill. Switching to LN subscription now. Happy babysitting, Canada. Azure Squadron out."

It took her all of 45 seconds to get an IM together and out to me through LN.

[You should know better than to try and bravado yourself out of the hand now, Javier. If you had two pair beat you never would have just called Knisse's check-raise. And if you think I won't have two pair beat, you really may have to find a side job for what you're gonna owe me!" - EPaulsen]

Nice thing about LN or Laser Net, is that it's so low-maintenance and benign no one cares about the traffic. Basically, the Canada is a LaserNet hub for all the ships assigned to her Battle Group(BG). All our ships, from the big to the small, subscribe to the Canada via directed comm laser over a network of computer-controlled autonomous connections, or CAC. The CAC network basically allows my Command Fighter to download real-time data from the Canada, who receives her data from the other ships of the Group and also direct from Earth. Her Command LaserNet to Earth allows the fleet Admiralty to carry on near-live conversations with Earth and piggybacks GI (Global Internet) access for the BG. Through my heads-up display, I could carry on several vidcomm, audcomm, or textcomm sessions with other members of the BG depending on my subscription parameters. The CAC even allows my fighter to use another closer ship in the Group as a relay in case I can't maintain a direct line to Canada.

So, while I discuss the poker hand with Major Paulsen via textcomm, I have the ability to review whatever available data is important to me. As a retired career combat pilot, most of my data can be broken down into 3 sections beyond the data of my own squadron and command:

Fighter Group Two's squadron information. I've often found it important to be aware of who's left that's friendly so I can either run with or run to them when things go sour. At my stage in combat expertise, I just use a graphic chart of fighters, one for each squadron commander. As their squadrons diminish, then their icon graphic starts to cover over in red indicating a loss roughly equivalent to their squadron. If the icon is white and the cell is 50% covered in red, then they've lost half their squadron. If the icon or their name is red, then their reporting damage or mayday data. If it goes black then we lost them. If both the name and the squadron fighter go black, then we lost both the squadron commander's ship and the person as well. Sounds cold and unfeeling. It is. Welcome to war. Tacticians of today would say that the bonus of this awareness is that the nearest squadron commander's fighter can assume the additional members of the fighter's squadron into their tactical network and the squadron isn't really lost nor is there going to be chaos of command.

The second area is Battle Group Two's tactical vessels beyond the fighters, with status and location. I can't begin to explain the complexity and hassles of navigating in space. First and foremost is the fact that space is truly three-dimensional. There are no basic poles to use North-South references. We do actually use such references, but it's all handled artificially. And then you have angles of inclination or declination with reference to either your ship or another source if using a reference. So, the computers talk back and forth updating direction and azimuth so that I can find a 200,000 metric ton needle in the stellar haystack. The funny part of all of this work, is that any vessel's heat or emission signature is so visible in the void of space, that I could just contact some kids on earth via the LN and ask them for directions if I needed to!

Which brings me to my third area. It's basically my own little custom display area. When I first used this type of tech on Earth at Boosaaso, I used map images in the square display area to to give me a hypersensitive overlay of the terrain so I knew where to ditch, head for cover, or lure in the enemy with the wounded bird trick. Out here, I use it to get the weather in San Pedro (Belize) so I can pretend I'm at home having a Sangria or Margarita. Today, though, I'm using it for near real-time updates from Canada's Media Relations creeps who are documenting everything so they can edit later and give the media back on Earth something dramatic, not boring like this is destined to be.

["Hey, I folded man. What'd you have?! You better have been able to beat my 5s with 20k in the pot!"-DLee] came up as Azure Squadron started our patrol, leaving our starting point or "station," slowly accelerating and scanning the void. The thrust silently shifted me back in my seat, like a warm blanket draped over you...

## III.

I woke up stuck to my clothing and lasciviously chewing on the soft coconut of the Mounds candy I had just been dreaming of. I was concerned at first that I had drooled all over myself, as opposed to just drenched with sweat, but that passed when I checked the system status and verified I had only fallen asleep and hadn't been ambushed by the imaginary Ceres rebel fleet! The reality to my 'sticky situation' (pun intended) was that I hadn't been awake when the humidity control system asked me if it should purge the water collector, so it didn't purge it. Instead, I was dreaming about the way my ace of spades and my king of diamonds fit so nicely with the flop in our poker game. The flop had been king of hearts, five of diamonds, and three of diamonds. I was on a roll. That part had been real. The part where I came back, we finished the hand, and I'd won twenty-thousand creds had been the dream, unfortunately.

Back to my high humidity issues. On a larger ship or vessel, the "dehumidifier" part of the air scrubbers reclaims the moisture in the air. It purifies and collects the water to recycle it and also to keep it away from the electronics. In a large ship, with a thousand personnel on board, humidity in the tin can will saturate every surface in a few hours just from the water humans give off through evaporation, perspiration, and breathing. That, as the earliest vessels found out, will wreak all kinds of hell on your systems. Unfortunately, a fighter, even a command fighter, is just a much smaller tin can. The issue here is that oxygen and space are very limited in tiny ships like fighters. So, the moisture collected into the water tank always outweighs the amount that I or just about any pilot will consume in the course of a mission which is why there is a purge on the tank 'to disperse excess liquid waste from the system in nano size ice dust' which is essentially harmless even to human spacecraft. This requires some oxygen, of course, for the purge. And since oxygen (and power to some degree) is scarce, we can't just have the system automatically purging liquid whenever it feels like it. What would happen if it were to error out and just keep auto-purging the the system and some O2 every time? Tragedy, according to the eggheads at home. Of course, because of the humidity and violent purpose of the fighter, all of the internal systems are sealed and coated so it's really just the pilot and anything they have or wear that gets saturated. And no matter what the eggheads say about the ultimate stay-dry superpower of our body-molded flight suits, wet material doesn't breathe worth a damn. Period. And yes, they probably ARE rocket scientists that believe what they're shoveling.

After waking from one of if not the only (and so secret everyone knows about it) probably court-martial-able perks of the Deep Patrol – the NAP - I pieced together the last two hours. I had spent the better part of an hour locked in a three-way battle of wits with Major Paulsen and Captain Lee – that is until Paulsen had reached her multitask limits and Lee actually launched. I remember being more confident that Major Ezera G Paulsen was actually trying so hard to BLUFF me into folding from out here that I knew she had been caught with her hand in the cookie jar. It's so sad when a traditionally very conservative ("tight") player overdoes a bluff because they're just not used to it. I had almost, almost, told her that I had "Big Slick" (ace/king hole cards for those uninitiated) when the flop came king of hearts with a five and three of diamonds. She may have had a king, but I bet it was more king/jack or something than the dominating hand I had. Of course, I didn't give her any information on my hand other than it was stronger than hers and she should give up her bluff. To which she judiciously noted that "People who snore shouldn't nap on Deep Patrol." While we may have enough history for her to know if I snore, I don't think I snore when I nap, and definitely not on patrol. Not in this moisture anyway, right? Darn it all.

Unfortunately, I didn't have the chance to labor over a clever retort as she was finally called away as the visitors to our little system were finally arriving, hours after the originally calculated time. Apparently the uber-eggheads were so excited to get light sabers from the Cylons they forgot that the aliens would have to decelerate in-system - just like we do - in order to not overshoot or run into obstacles such as solar system bodies and asteroids or those pesky planets. Apparently the new rendezvous was going to be just past Mars' solar orbit and a little bit closer to me at the end of my patrol. Hooray! I may actually get to be present for the greatest event in human history!

I began to manually review and verify random data and observations of the two fighter flights just to make sure that the Brains didn't mess anything up. So far, they never really have had errors, but I always think it's good to double-check things on my own - no matter how much faster or reliable the computer is.

Almost an hour of banter, followed by an almost forty minute power-nap, with only about half an hour left which flew by while I was reviewing and recalculating assumptions that took the computer one-tenth of a second to figure out, and now the chance to see the alien fleet with my own eyes. Things were really looking up! I'll bet Lee had a 6-5 or a 7-6 which is why he stuck around until the turn but then bailed when the straight never came or his pair of 5s looked too weak to stick around. Hmm - I wonder if Paulsen has Jack-7 of diamonds and has too many outs to get out of the hand?

*** 

As the ships of my squadron came together for our formation to return home, I was again reminded of how unassuming and unremarkable space-fighters were. Even these newer X-4 designs, while slightly more interesting than the X-3 Saucer design, are still quite plain looking. It was easy to explain to others about the 'flying saucer' look of the X-3. They literally were flying discs with a variety of maneuvering thrusters mounted around the disk and had no visibly distinguishable front end. Well, until you added the two additional weapon/fuel pods which earned them the nickname the "Mickeys" in full load. Mainly because, from the top, they looked like the Mickey Mouse outline.

These new fighters, though, are basically flying diamonds or kite-shaped fighters. With the long nose and low profiles from all sides, they are really very sleek with the only large profile being the top or bottom. In combat, the idea is that as you move toward an enemy your much harder to discern through targeting lock and visual scanning. As well, with the smaller profile you're supposed to be harder to hit. Another advantage is that strikes are more likely to deflect somewhat due to the deflecting angle of the hull. And if you pass or turn away from your target, the key is to remember to turn left or right, so you always present a very small target. While these have never been really battle-tested, the riskiest time in an X-3 was when a rookie pilot would 'pull up' from an attack vector and present a nice big round target allowing the enemy to put a few plasma strikes right between Mickey's ears.

Another nice thing is the 'plows' on these fighters. The flying diamond is great, but the addition of basic carbon nano-mesh reflective plows on the front edges of the diamond allow not only enemy fire to be deflected away but allow any micro-debris and hazards of combat to be deflected away [hopefully] harmlessly. Even more interesting and hopefully never necessary; the plows are actually somewhat wing-shaped and can retract back and outward to lock in for in-atmosphere, yet extremely limited, "descent control." Basically, after you get through the outer atmosphere of a planet, you can use the plows as wings to turn your falling rock into a slightly controlled landing rock. In principle and in simulators, they work very well to allow you to maneuver to where you'd like to crash your fighter, literally. And I mean crash – these diamond babies don't actually have any landing gear!

Diamonds. There were two diamonds on the flop. King of hearts with the five and three of diamonds now that I think of it. Maybe Lee was lying and really folded a diamond flush draw? Hmm. Or maybe he really did have 5s and made the right call to get out. I'll bet Paulsen has the diamond flush draw. She's probably banking on her reputation as a tight player and the eight cards she could catch to complete it.

## IV.

*<Lee's making a run at the main enemy vessel, Ortiz. If you get here in time, he could use the help or even a distraction from your side to maybe give him a window.>* How the hell had we come to this?! Are humans so naive that we can't even MEET an alien species without war? Stop. I needed to focus and get my mind on my tasks, work the solution not how we got here. I heard an explosion in the background at her end and lost Paulsen on audcomm. Canada was still on my grid, so hopefully it was just minor damage or not even combat damage at all. The grid is the current name for the Laser Detection Grid, which is basically the modern version of old-school radar but in three dimensions for spacecraft. Basically your laser sensors can pinpoint objects detected by scanners and analyze them for data and near-realtime updates. This all gets plotted on a 3D display which helps you figure out your position relative to all other items. And the further away you are the more important the 'relative' in that matters. In a 2D system, you could head toward the carrier, for example, and end up overlapping the same spot in the display. BUT, because your approach was let's say fifteen degrees below (or above) it from where you started 1.2 million kilometers away, you'd end up about 320,000 kilometers away from the target. Or roughly eight times the circumference of the earth. That's a big haystack when you're looking for that needle.

I hope she's okay and had her suit on at least. Paulsen was good, but sometimes she knew too well how good she was and her overconfidence got the better of her. She better have brought her helmet into CIC with her or I was gonna have to kick her ass when I got back!

"Cerb, send the following message to Captain Lee, Rogue two, encryption package three, with the point I'm designating strike 1, mark. "Lee, Ortiz here. I'm en-route and should be able to assist your efforts with a distraction from starboard and stern, in three point...two minutes; now, now, now. If you can hold your run or rendezvous at the reference point attached we can give these bastards hell they'll never forget. Ortiz out. Mark. Send it, Cerb!"

Cerb is the combat AI for my Command Fighter, Cerberus One, as I've named him. Cerb and I have spent a lot of time in training together prior to ever coming out here, so there's no question about him understanding just about anything I may tell him. All pilots in space spend months prior to deployment training with their AI counterparts in order to ensure that they are able to operate within acceptable levels of strain or stress. Cerb is actually an update of my on-Earth AI, modified for this new gig, so we had less shake-out time than normal. Most of that was spent with new terminology and how I would communicate certain things. I have about a dozen versions and copies of Cerb on several data blocks on the Canada and at home. It's the pilot's job, usually, to have the AI available in case they get plugged into a different vessel during combat situations. Nothing worse than hopping in the only available fighter and not being able to tell the damned thing to start up because you don't speak Cantonese or don't know what the last person called the 'engines' in their own little world. I know, makes it complicated, but this way the pilot makes the tech work with him more cohesively, not just for him. The results have been astounding over the last 20+ years of using this method. Combat effectiveness is nearly 40% better than any alternative. With the new software setting that standard to shame. Cerb 3.6 here is the newest version.

I switched back to trying to get the Canada on audcomm. I had about three minutes now before I had to deploy in combat formation and I needed answers as to what was going on. All hell had broke loose about one relative minute ago.

I could audcomm the rest of the fighters, but armchair quarterbacking from outside the combat zone was the kind of thing every fighter jock despised – someone sitting in a nice place out of the fight trying to 'help' but really only just irritating everyone.

Fighters were now launching from Canada faster than we'd ever practiced or predicted in the simulators. Yet vessels of all types were blinking out of existence on my CAC at an alarming rate! The Myanmar, a destroyer from the Pacific Nation, was the second capital vessel to blink out of existence.

What the hell happened? I started to review combat scenarios and tried not to watch the ship life indicators blink cold while I was still useless for over two more minutes.

As I had approached on my return vector, at roughly nine percent of light speed, I had a nice sensor read on the situation as everything was playing out over CAC for me. All appeared to be going as well as could be hoped. The Canada's battle group was about one-hundred thousand kilometers from the alien fleet and at a near stop. The alien fleet was also at a crawl approaching them. Both appeared to be deployed in a defensive formation with several screening vessels between them but in close to their main ships. Communications had been established and the aliens had agreed somehow to send an envoy to the Canada for what was effectively a parley or maybe a meeting to establish peaceful relations. The Winston Churchill battleship, built in the European Union, was sending her delegation as well. She served as the Flag Bridge for the fleet Admiralty - there just wasn't enough room to really have both operations on the same vessel – and was sending what sounded like the entire Flag staff. The WC's battle group was effectively standing next to the Canada's battle group, crawling along at a near stop as well. The readings indicate that the mammoth alien vessel launched their shuttle, if that's what it would be called, which jumped to .1c (10% speed of light) before it had cleared the gigantic ship's side. It was at nearly .2c, twice the max speed of my X-4 fighter, when it exploded next to the destroyer Illinois at a range of about twenty kilometers. All my data seemed to indicate that the Illinois destroyed it as soon as it hit her inner envelope with a combined plasma and laser attack. Was it political? Sabotage? Did they know something the rest of us haven't discovered yet? What I do know is that the alien main vessel, easily twenty times the mass of the Canada's battle group, launched a series of what I would call missiles which blew the Illinois into pieces and then blew up those pieces in alphabetical order! If there's anything left of the black box in the few thousand pieces of rubble the ship was reduced to, maybe someday we'll have answers of what happened. As I had watched the readout show the destruction of the Illinois and update navigation with all the new threats, Cerb updated me that the main ship had launched a dozen small craft which were headed toward the Earth fleets.

That had now been two minutes ago.

\*\*\*

Thirty seconds out I was reviewing the updates as they came in over the CAC, and so far the battle was hideously one-sided. The twelve alien "bombers" as the system was now calling them, in spite of their mass only about two-thirds that of a destroyer-class earth vessel, had reduced the forward screening elements of the Canada's battle group to husks of space-rock and were now engaging the Winston Churchill's battle fleet at nearly point-blank range. As just the larger combat vessels, WC's battle group didn't have many screening vessels. She had two heavy cruisers and two light cruisers, one each from the AR(Asian Republic) and the PN(Pacific Nations) shipyards. With the SADR (South American Democratic Republic) battleship Chile along-side, the WC had a total of six heavy-hitting vessels of destruction which we would have thrown at any alien (or human for that matter) force that wasn't smart enough to bow in awe at the site of those vessels. I remember Carter wanted to call the Winston Churchill or the Chile something like SDF One or Super Defense Fort or something like that. Probably would have made sense, considering humanity's arrogance over the accomplishments.

It's hard to take solace in the knowledge you gain from watching a new foe surgically dismantle the most powerful vessels of your species' arsenal. Unfortunately I, like the rest of the fleet, was learning quite a bit as the alien "bombers" destroyed the cruiser Papua and tore through the defenses of the Chile with a disturbing rhythm and efficiency that chilled my sweat-soaked spine and set my mind ablaze searching for ways to adapt and overcome their defenses. The Chile didn't go out without a fight, though.

&lt;Ortiz, this is Canada. What's your situation?&gt;

The Chile, learning from her first salvo that her individual laser and plasma weapons weren't able to penetrate what could only be called shields of several bombers at once, concentrated a series of laser and plasma bursts on the lead alien bomber. While the lasers seemed easily dissipated, I guess, by the shields, they seemed to have further issues with plasma weapons and the concentration of several were able to overcome or overload the shield and tore holes through the alien bomber. It bucked and listed as plasma scorched across its surface and some sort of atmosphere spewed out of its starboard or right side where the Chile had annihilated that half of the vessel.

"Paulsen, glad to hear you're alright. We're inbound on alien primary vessel at max speed with an eta of one-zero-three seconds. Sent word to Lee to rendezvous for alien counterattack. Trying to analyze enemy data but it's looking pretty premature at best. Designate 'bomber' class vessels appear to have some sort of compressed plasma pulse weapon which is nearly bypassing point defense and allowing successful direct hits. Each vessel is demonstrating double the X-4 fighter speed with only slightly negligible maneuverability. And the bastards have some sort of atmosphere. Confirm. Over."

The other eleven "bombers" split in four directions but twisted their orientation until they were able to fire a concentrated attack from all eleven against a small area on the bow of the Chile with their forward firing arsenals, basically immolating what must have been a forward missile bay as several small explosions blew out that same area further damaging the hull. Luckily, missile ordnance is relatively stable while safeties are engaged prior to launch. IF that holds any real comfort as people starve for oxygen or die in explosions of fire or electricity.

"Commander" came the AI voice assigned for Cerb, " Squadron Commander Captain Nguyen is gone. His squadron is at about one third original numbers. I can acquire the remaining vessels for addition to our battle capacity in twelve seconds if you wish." Cerb's voice has always been a cold and calculating sound to me. It irritates me in combat, seemingly uncaring (which it is) but reminds me I have a job to do and don't have the luxury of grief just yet. And in forty-two seconds, I'll be another pilot in humanity's first meeting with an extrasolar alien species – where I'm going to have to kill them all or die trying. Nguyen had folded pre-flop in our game before we got scrambled. I guess there are things worse than Deep Patrol.

I shall be immortal.

<Javier, Canada. Confirmed on alien assessment. Wynne suggests concentrated attacks to presumably weaker areas such as rear sections or obvious hull seams and such. We're analyzing the atmosphere from that fighter but it's really bottom priority at the moment. We have some egg-heads in the observatory lab trying to gather data in order to give us an advantage. Admiral Nutomo is going to take the WC's BG toward the enemy main vessel, designation "AV1", in an attempt to not only destroy it but lead the bombers away from Canada so we can retreat to a safer zone outside of the combat area and continue to fight from maximum fighter ranges in order to maximize our potential strike capabilities and wear down their defenses. Chile is already launching lifeboats and has aligned for a collision in case they completely lose ship function. We've sent the destroyers Torah and Shiva ahead of Nutomo's command in order to screen her approach to the AV1, if even possible, and ascertain her fighting prowess.*

It's not looking good, Javier. We've lost over a third of our fighters and none of us have gone near that behemoth sitting out there. If it has weapons even close to what its scale suggests, then Wynne thinks we should use fighters to evaluate prior to capital ship engagement. We're rearming with mainly anti-fighter ordnance in order to stop those bombers. They could overtake us pretty quickly if they get past the frigates watching our backside as we run. You going to be okay with what you've got out there? Has Cerb come up with any save-the-day scenarios I should know about?>* She chuckled at her own joke. Her voice was strong and only showed a little bit of shakiness she must be feeling as the proverbial stuff is hitting the fan. I hadn't realized until the end that the whole audcomm had been private. I'll bet she has a diamond flush draw.

"Cerb, acquire Nguyen's squadron. When we get into position; patch me into all fighter-based comms and keep separate indicators for Canada, Paulsen, Flag traffic, Nutomo and the X-4 squadrons. Monitor the band for anything you think is pertinent and forward that to me as well. Then, plot an intercept course for Canada and execute an elliptical pass along the enemy vessel which will minimize our exposure to return turret fire and maximize damage. Follow that with a way to keep the sun at our backs if we make a second pass. Hopefully that will blind them so that we can hit something vital. Continue with that pattern until the bombers become a threat, range increment 2. And monitor the combat damage of the Winston Churchill and analyze for ways we may be able to assist."

I punched up Combat View, or CView, which turns the core of the fighter into a virtual observation platform as if the walls were just windows displaying the outside of the ship. Most fighter pilots prefer TacView which gives them something more like the bubble-top view of a fighter, keeping them more grounded in the cockpit with a seat-of-your-pants feel. It's really all electronic sensors displayed on the walls of the core, which is basically like the inside of an LED video sphere, so it doesn't actually have an effect other than in your head. If the G-forces were no longer an issue, you could fly backwards into combat but be viewing everything as if you were facing forward. Gravity changes make the bumps and zigs a little disorienting though, but the combat implications are tremendous. We often train to "slide" along a larger vessel firing weapons and altering our course up or down as we travel sideways. And the concept of being chased practically becomes nonexistent – as you could move 'forward' and flip over your ship to face backwards while still moving in the same direction, now backward. This means that all an enemy is doing, then, is getting closer to your 'forward' weapons.

"Captain Nguyen's squadron now subscribed and on approach to the rendezvous point. I've selected Anti-ship formation and labeled the flight as "Medusa," sir. It should minimize our personal exposure but allow Minotaur flight to strike hard at targets of opportunity with the Gauss cannons. I thought it would be nice to test the GC18 in combat. Plus I've analyzed the shields of the enemy and have not found them to have been tested with projectile weapons. I also expect a one hundred percent target hit, given the range and overwhelming size of the enemy vessel...."

"Cerb, shut up. Medusa approved. How about you find a way to disable their shields or hurt them instead of yakking my ears off?"

"Nice name, Medusa, sir. I'm sure the irony would not be lost on the enemy if they knew you, sir." Cerb, like Paulsen, had a way with words. You give an AI a little personality and the first thing they understand is sarcasm. If I knew anything about software I'd swear that the nerds at Academy who design these put that in there on purpose.

In CView, you basically have a HUD and dimmed touch controls displayed on whatever screen you want, in whatever configuration. The advantage, to me, is that as an old man I like to see everything! So I give up the cockpit feel with the nose running out in front of me for something that lets me see all around me. It's like flying in an invisible plane, if that makes any sense.

Cerb can also make changes to the displays or even in-flight controls as needed. It takes some getting used to, but the AIs are so quick at processing ALL the data in the sensors, that he'll process a missile on my tail and zig when it fires or hit it with point defense. He could even flip the ship over and hit it with a direct weapon if wished! He'll tell me as he does it, but it's really just a courtesy programmed in by the egg-heads who think the AIs should really do it all alone anyway. It takes years to develop a team approach that works as well as ours does, but sometimes the human really is a liability to the AI, which wants to 'live' just as much as we do.

"Cerb, patch me to Major Paulsen's private audcomm channel. Her ears only."

Ten seconds and I'd be right in the thick of things. Laughing along in my invisible fighter. For some reason, I don't really appreciate the idea that I'm Wonder Woman.

# V.

Cerb slowed our X-4 to just under .001c or one thousandth of light speed. It sounds slow, but it's still racing along at 300 kilometers a second. That means we'd make it from New York, NAF to London, EU in about 18 seconds. If I blinked for half a second, which happens without artificial eyes, I'd miss 150 kilometers of the ocean. That means I could miss a convoy of over 300 turn-of-the-century nuclear aircraft carriers from the former United States Navy, if they were traveling with about 300 meters between each one and traveling end-to-end. That's a lot to miss. However, we aren't close enough yet for it to matter, but very soon we'll be down around .0001c which puts us around 30km per second. The math is pretty easy if you figure the speed of light is 300,000km per second.

*<I'm awful busy, Ortiz. Kinda got an interstellar war going on here, which, when you get in the fight, you'll notice is going well for the enemy. I'm not going to tell you what my hand in the game is until you get back here after kicking some alien butt outta our system! So, what do you want that needs a private channel? Over.>*

Six X-4 fighters dropped in on my right flank and I realized that Lee had made his way here by taking a swipe or two at the enemy en-route. He had lost seven of his twelve fighters it seemed, with some minor damage popping up every second as Cerb brought their data into my assessment view.

"Hold on Ezera."

I switched to comm Captain David Lee, European Union hero, and all-around good guy. He had comm'd me earlier wondering what I'd had in our poker game prior to coming out here. I felt bad for him, if it was true he only had made a pair of fives in our last, and yet unfinished, hand. He was a good poker player but too loose with his creds and had dumped 300 with the pre-flop betting. Followed by 600 after the king of hearts, five and three of diamonds came on the flop when he called the rest of our bets. Still, he was an excellent pilot so I guess it's better to have that going for you than always making the right call in poker. "I'm on with Paulsen who won't admit she's just got a flush draw and should fold. Give Cerb any insight you and Han – yes, his AI is named Han – have on what you've observed. That is one enormous pig of a ship for us to bring down. Out."

"Hey, when she admits it tell her I'm laughing at her calling Knisse's 5000 cred raise on you after that second king came up. Even I am not crazy enough to call 5k on a draw. Out" Lee was right, he WAS crazy. But in this kind of situation I wanted his outside-the-box thinking more than I wanted a battleship instead of a fighter. Okay, maybe the battleship would be better. Cerb started updating points of interest on the tactical window of AV1, with some especially juicy looking power node points that might be defensive nodes for their shields.

"Paulsen. Ortiz."

*<Really? I thought someone else had me on hold in the middle of a freakin' war. Out>*

"Lee says he's laughing at you for calling with just a diamond draw. He says even he's not THAT crazy. And face it, he IS that crazy."

*<Talking about the hand while it's still going on or sharing card information can disqualify the hand. Y'all just made me a rich bitch, thanks! When we get out of this I'll be sure to gloat some more.>* She issued several orders in the background while I watched my surroundings update with targets, designations, new Operational Coordinates (OpCos) for reference, and the fact that several fighter squadrons were missing with only a dim marker of last-known coordinates. Problem was, there weren't any enemy vessels near them. Except (DAMN!) for the supposedly disabled enemy bomber, still tagged as disabled and a non-threat.

I flipped open comm traffic. "Fleet, Ortiz here. Avoid Bogey Bomber 1. Propulsion may be down but weapons are still active. Marking target and estimated range of weapons fire." Cerb already had it up before I said it, but it was good form, again, when he told me.

*<Good find, Azure Squadron. Now, Ortiz, how about you and Rogue squadron get your asses in gear and bring that big mother*

*down? I've got an eighteen year bottle of single-malt for each of you to celebrate when you get back to Canada afterward. Paid for by Ortiz and Knisse, my favorite poker suckers! Paulsen out.>*

Suddenly the visual display dimmed as a large fireball – oxygen burns temporarily in space – exploded close enough for us to worry about debris and pieces larger than point defense could handle.

It was the Chile – she had gotten close enough to begin firing on AV1 and while I was chatting away foolishly about poker she was going toe-to-toe with a ship easily twenty times her mass and using technology we were recently imagining for science fiction.

*<In nomine patris, et filii...>* Lee started a prayer for the ship and anyone left on board. Even with them launching lifeboats en route, it looks like only a third of the 2100 souls could have gotten off before she went Nova. Her Nova buoy, which marked her black box and had all of her data logs sprang to life and headed toward Earth.

"Han and I have evaluated the demise of the Chile and ascertained several points of interest in the alien vessel. We are ready to make a coordinated strike. I have taken the liberty of assuming we will stay in Medusa formation and precede Rogue squadron to screen them from further losses, as they are at 41% of combat effectiveness. " It was Cerb, back to business.

Watching the Chile's demise and listening to Cerb, for some reason, reminded me that it's just as important to watch someone fold in Poker as it is to watch them win. You look for tells. You look for patterns. It's the same in any combat or strategic exercise, like human sports, as it is in warfare: You must observe and learn all things from your foes, not just their victory. For if you only learn about their victory, you'll never believe they can lose. Sounds very Sun Tzu, but I've never really been one to quote well.

I hope Bob Nguyen enjoyed our Hold'em games.

\*\*\*

We started our attack run along the long elliptic of the gargantuan AV1 vessel. At first, I thought she figured we were too insignificant to care about, until Han and Cerb suddenly updated energy activity across the side of the ship. As we slid along her and came within medium range, we unleashed a barrage of heavy fire at her stern and headed toward her bow.

My X-4C Command Fighter and the other eight fighters under my command, now twelve with Nguyen's flight added, were physically no different in size, shape, energy signature, or even physical structures. Yeah, we may paint them or mark them for visual numbering, but like most everything else in humanity they weren't really that distinguishable from one another. The real difference, though, was inside. The Command Fighter gave up an internal ordnance bay and redundant combat system in order to accommodate a human pilot in the Core that was, essentially, the cockpit of the modern space-fighter. The Core was just a hollow ball that could actually be moved modularly from any X-4 to another X-4. All you had to do was remove the ORS – Ordnance and Redundant System – module and you could swap in the Command Core or Core. The main reason for this was that in early combat it was known to take the Commander out of the fight first, so it became the target of ALL enemy fire until it was brought down. And no ship was built to decently survive heavy concentrated fire from several comparable vessels or larger. So, since before a space-fighter really was in service, it was always important that the Core ship always be indistinguishable from the others – because so far Command agreed that a human on-site was still the best choice for combat operations. And I agreed wholeheartedly with them.

The rest of the squadron, though, were all dumbed-down AIs. Cerb preferred the term "second cousin" or just "cousin" ever since I had explained how mine were. Not sure if that says much for them, but they're probably a lot smarter than ANY of my cousins. I had two flights with me, four fully armed fighters in each flight. The ordnance was always the concern though. I had outfitted for several scenarios, but mostly anti-fighter roles since I didn't really figure to have to go against that vessel before I ever got back to the Canada and rearmed. Honestly, I had really thought we were totally screwed if it came to a fight with interstellar aliens who just traveled across our Galaxy from the other side. Since we were just starting to dance in our own little corner of the world.

We increased lateral, or basically sideways speed, and Minotaur Flight began unloading their four Gauss cannons at the alien Vessel's side. Some of the projectiles appeared to get through, as Cerb had predicted, until they'd spent their limited ammunition supplies. Projectiles took mass and created small but not ineffectual recoil when fired. A ship can really only reasonably carry so much - and since these had never been tested in a real combat, a full payload would have been a poor choice in the case of fighter combat. It was unfortunate that they were actually effective. Gorgon Flight followed with pulsed plasma cannon fire as Cerb had recommended and met less, but still some limited success. With Nguyen and Lee's squadron remnants following along with the same pattern, we actually seemed to plasma burn a lengthy section of the AV1's hull, glaringly obvious in the light of our system's sun.

Another fireball, this one a little closer than I would have liked, lit up the dark around us. Apparently one of the heavy cruisers in the Admiral's BG had succumbed to bomber fire. As I checked the updates I noticed that the bombers broke off of the capital ships and headed for some little green specks on the plot. We were those little green specks, apparently annoying someone on the mother ship.

"Good" I said into the open mic. "About time someone recognized us for ass-kickers and heart-breakers! Well, if these things had hearts or asses, I suppose. 10 seconds. Lee, let's slip back around the other side of AV1 and maybe roll around her as we teach these bastards how to fight in space?!"

I checked my tactical information and comm'd the Canada CIC.

"Hey Paulsen. You taking notes? Notice no bluff here. No diamond draw. Just those of us with a hand worth playing!"

*<How 'bout I demonstrate a real playing hand, you ass. It's about time you learned what kind of woman you're dealing with. Maybe next time you see me you'll remember this bitch has bite. And not the kind you're thinking of, jerk!>* The next second was a beautiful image on my CView. The Canada was the center of an explosion of green as she flushed the fighters I was "missing" from my view. I'd thought most had been destroyed, but I guess Canada was just rearming them! It was truly a heartwarming moment that gave me hope.

*<How's that for a flush draw, Ortiz?>*

*<God that's a beautiful site to behold, eh Colonel?>* came Lee's admiration. Apparently he saw the same thing I did.

My fighter jerked hard in what would have been up and backward if it had meaning out here, as Cerb asked "would you like a drink with the show, sir? Or perhaps we should address the issue of eleven bombers trying to make us a pretty explosion in space?" Only Cerb can make saving my bacon sound like a waste of someone's time.

"Shut it Cerb! Let's get these things one at a time using Minotaur as the draw and Gorgon flight to concentrate on a single target. You and I will be the two-punch to Lee's squadron's one-punch with Nguyen's squad remnant to back us up and cover. Got it?" I yelled as we continued to evade incoming fire and opened up our formation a little so no one bounced off one another.

Cerb agreed and we pushed the Minotaur fighters out a little toward the bombers as our entire squadron and the enemy circled in a slow arc around the enemy main vessel. It would cause them to be more cautious about their targeting and hopefully keep them a little distracted as Gorgon flight drifted out and away.

Now that we were in fighter combat I turned on the sound approximators – which was the egg-head way of saying speakers in the fighter which made sounds based on the sensor readings as they happened. Space is silent. There's nothing out here to notice when someone isn't in view, so the SAFS (Sound Approximation Fighter System) units were created to once again help pilots to process multiple pieces of data beyond just visual. Now, if a ship were to fire on me from behind me, the speaker(s) in that area would mimic the associated sound for laser or gun fire. At first, it's quite ridiculous, as the uber-eggheads of course used Star Wars hokey sounds for a lot of effects. Thus, if another ship went flying by, you heard the tell-tale sign of a passing Tie Fighter sound. If someone fired projectile weapons, you'd hear machine gun fire from that direction. This way, I didn't have to see plasma blasts as they went by, I could hear the direction and do what I had to do.

"Lee, we're gonna take out bomber 4 it looks like first with concentrated plasma fire. We're gonna take his five buddies down the left side. Now!" I yelled into the mic again, a primal yell as I willed the shredding of bomber four apart - just as the six bombers headed for Minotaur flight. I was screaming so maniacally in my exultation at bomber 4 crumbling, in fact, that I took Lee's own yelling to be bloody approval as bomber 4 died perhaps too easily. But I figured out what his real concerns were when his fighter and two others from his squadron exploded right on the other side of Stheno1, one of my Gorgon flight fighters. Stheno screened us from debris, fortunately, but was shredded herself with the loss of Lee's squadron and the onslaught of passing fire from the second bomber group.

Apparently the enemy had thought about a similar maneuver to ours, and as we were focusing on bomber 4, which still streamed atmosphere and fluids of some sort, the other five bombers had flanked us on Lee's side and slid in for the kill.

As we reoriented, Cerb and I took the rest of Gorgon flight and Lee's remaining two fighters with us after the five that had just crossed our paths. We hard accelerated toward them coming up on their respective tails. As the six of us concentrated on Bomber 7, trailing slightly behind, we found that their shields were well capable of blocking most of our plasma fire. Luckily the pulse effect Cerb had hypothesized was able to overload the shields they used and we were able to cause some devastation to the aft corner, blowing out one of the main engines. As it rolled over to bear its weapons on us, I was able to get a better look at it. It was large, probably three times the mass of an X-4 fighter, and very boxy and squat. It had a snub nose on its heart-shaped 'face' in front with a large opening that looked like a round mouth. It was probably the deadly beam weapon they were using to slice up our fleet. It had wings that came out of the top and hunched over and forward, probably for defensive shielding and added weapons capacity. The engine nozzles were fairly normal-looking, almost like old jet engine nozzles except these were shielded and allowed it to easily move at speeds we weren't even close to reaching yet. It had a menacing, almost feral look to it, like the face of a baboon with deadly intent. And that's what I started laughing about. The deadly baboons tearing up our fleet. And it gave them a kind of face for me to focus on when the laughing quit and I realized that Lee was never going to make poker again. And I made sure Bomber 7 paid the price for their transgressions as their group split apart and they all shot off in different directions.

***

"Cerb, I want you to figure out how many PCs we need to overcome their shields with the time and pulse efficiency needed to take one of those things out. Once you've got that, analyze their patterns and see if you can figure out their target selections or other patterns to how they're evaluating targets." They've taken out a battleship and some heavy cruisers, then gone against fighters, run all over a couple destroyers, and then gone back to fighters. Damned peculiar strategy. "Bring up..." One of Lee's fighters exploded and Cerb jerked our ship and surrounding vessels into a ninety degree change of face and then jumped to full acceleration, which thumped me right good in the Core as I was trying to look around and see what hit us. I couldn't see anything...and then I noticed that the rear third of my inner Core viewers weren't changing over my right shoulder. Damn, they must have come in from my blind side. It also meant that if Cerb hadn't reacted, the sensors must have been damaged not just the internal screens. And no one else said anything, either... that is just downright frightening like you can't believe. There is no way to do stealth in space. They didn't have anything like it inbound, so it's doubtful they have something like it here. They're not THAT far ahead of us that they could have something like that. So what the hell was it?!

Now I could see them, the larger group having amassed seven of the nine bombers left. I cut into a weave, well as much as you can in space. It's really more like a bunch of hops up or down left or right with radical changes in direction. The drones maneuver far far better than I do, since they don't have the meat puppet (that's me) issue dealing with G forces. Problem is, they still don't reason well or have quite the unassisted killer instinct. And that's the way we humans like it. I myself have seen far too many "AIs take over the human race" vids to go against society on that topic. Plus, I know what the smart ones are like. If you added a little sinister to Cerb, I don't know what could stop him.

"Cerb, get some sort of repairs going on the sensors. Bring one of the fighters up in close formation if you have to and use theirs. We need to see what's out there..." I continued to bark orders to keep my mind off of Lee getting toasted. "Once that is fixed, figure out what happened back there." I noticed that the bombers were spreading out and looked to come in at me in a swarm from several directions at once. There were six of us left in our grouping, but a hailstorm of other fighters inbound in about forty seconds at the reasonable speeds they were traveling. I think they could have been here sooner, but they must have been waiting for something. I accelerated toward them on a parabolic intercept course. If this goes the way it looks, they'll be here just in time to get these guys as they finish me off. Well I'm not having ANY of that!

"Cerb, have what's left of Gorgon, Lee's, or Nguyen's fighters with mines or ordnance we can remote-detonate drop back some and drop those mines along our current course." I started typing points and command codes into the ship and running a few timing numbers.

"Is there a plan I should be aware of? They're really coming at us from everywhere BUT behind sir. I don't see how cutting off our only avenue of retreat..." Cerb trailed off when his CPUs got the analysis of what I was doing based on the numbers I was running. "Sometimes, sir, I'm not sure I envy your human ingenuity or if it scares me too much to want to know how you come up with this kind of thing." We finished the next ten seconds in silence until Cerb chimed in with his customary wit "If this works, it will be a miracle. If not, I suppose we at least take some of them with us. Just for the record, sir, there's still time to accelerate hard toward Canada and draw them toward the rest of the fighters and the anti-fighter guns on Canada? Before we get killed. "

The enemy was laying an elaborate trap. And I was the bait. I noticed from their pattern that their attack vectors when they came in would kill us or most of us and spit them out on perpendicular vectors to the incoming fighters if any got here at speed in time to be a factor. Then, they'd just swing back and forth a pass or two and wipe out several fighters before they could mass enough firepower to follow them. Back and forth at least once or twice, then they would be that much closer to Canada and have the fighters headed away from her. Plus, we'd be dead and a bunch of fighters squadrons would be easier targets until they massed at my current intercept point. Well, rather than feed the flies to the spiders – I decided that their ships look like squat spiders from the front – I'm going to make the spiders play my way.

I initiated command to flip my fighter around and started decelerating backward faster than I really should. The rest of the fighters slowed but continued on their course. This may or may not have confused the enemy, but they did nothing at my maneuver. I had Cerb go to full accel, so much that even the dampers in the X-4 weren't going to help compensate enough to keep me awake. I was buried into the seat practically, as I could feel my body compress and my vision quickly faded to black as the last thing I could see was the TacView showing the rest of my motley squad flipping and performing a similar maneuver.

\*\*\*

I was sitting at the poker table, looking at a pile of creds on the table. Nguyen and Lee were sitting across from me, smiling at their hands. The flop I remember, the king of hearts, five and three of diamonds, were there on the table. The turn was there too, with the king of spades. I looked over at Paulsen, lovely as ever with her hair tussled and highlighted by the heavenly light all around, as she showed her two diamonds and her flush draw. Okay, that's a bunch of bull. I didn't see a damned thing. No lights, no nothing. I just blacked out and I didn't see nor experience anything. Well, other than a damned headache as I came to.

We were accelerating hard. I must have been out for about four or five seconds as we were almost upon our mines now. The alien bombers had apparently taken my bait and came in on us hard. I figure they should overtake us just as we reach the mines, almost ideally according to plan. The mines weren't active, of course, otherwise we'd be blowing up before the bombers got near us! But I don't think they knew how they worked, because they were barreling in on us fast and didn't seem to even be interested in avoiding the mines nor taking evasive maneuvers in case of a trap.

You see, as we were headed for Canada and our saviors, they had fanned out around us and I believe were planning to streak in when the fighters were getting close and all bunched up to help and cover us. Or worse, when they were at their zero movement point if they tried to fall in with us in the opposite direction. Either way, win for the bombers. BUT, what I did by turning back toward the deep dark was to force them to choose to sit out there exposed, or to come in after me before my friends got here and we were all moving in the same direction. By turning tail, so to speak, they were robbed of their trap and not very happy about it I'd gathered.

For me, though, I've got almost enough room that if I time it right, the mines will blow up right on them after I pass them. Then, not only will they be somewhat grouped together, they'll be running from our fleet and right into my mines. If, that is, I don't get my whole squad killed in this hair-brained maneuver.

Plus, in all honesty, it is unlikely I'll be able to take out even one of them this way. The mines aren't very strong and don't really have the ability to do sustained pulses or prolonged engagements. They'll fire then explode after moving in on the enemy. Or us, if we're too close. Again, had I known we were going to be fighting like this, I would have planned for better programmable warheads on those. Ah hell; Actually, I would've taken sick leave or vacation and headed for earth so I could die in peace on the beach or something. Maybe.

The good news here is that I'm pulling them away from what's left of our fleet and the Canada, and into the straight-on sites of my fellow fighter squadrons. If I can disrupt even one or two of them, it goes a long way to keeping our entire force from being annihilated.

There's nothing worse than wondering if someone can hear you think. My plan was working perfectly. No one comm'd us with any direct communications for fear of reminding the aliens they were back there. As we almost hit the mines Cerb activated them and the hoard of nine bombers railed into them, mines firing pulsed plasma and laser weapons and eventually exploding all over the area behind us as the bombers made minor evasive maneuvers to avoid direct collisions with exploding balls of energy. Out of the field of explosions one bomber rolled forward listing slightly toward us as it was caught by several simultaneous hits and exploding mines, clearly having issues with course controls. Then right behind it two more leaped over the stumbling craft and right into our tail guns as they forged into our rear threat range. Unfortunately, they were far less damaged as we just didn't have the mines to saturate the area well.

And then they barreled forward accelerating at their amazing rate, headed right for us. I had hoped that they'd choose to evade and separate allowing our incoming fighters to lock onto a few and thin their ranks to something remotely manageable. Instead, our squads had to settle for the listing bomber and they tore away at it, like a swarm of killer bees taking small pieces out of a large predator. And that's what they were, larger ships than ours, more maneuverable, and better weapons and targeting controls. I think one good thing for us was that they didn't seem to know, yet, how fragile our ships truly were. Otherwise they wouldn't choose to swarm our fighters with so many of their own vessels. Or maybe they would – who's to say what alien space warfare tactics should be. Maybe they operate as a hive mind and can only attack one target. Or maybe they have a bunch of vessels slaved to one ship like we do so they are limited. Of course, if that's the case, I hope they only have one fighter squadron.

As they came into near point blank range Cerb shot our remaining fighters into a bloom in several directions away from the alien horde and brought all our front profiles to bear on the lead ship, firing as they blew past us. We had several hits, but they were grazing shots as our movement and the aliens uncanny acceleration and lateral movements kept us from being able to keep a good lock on them with the plasma cannons. I think we did some damage, but not enough to really bring it down. There were six of them blasting through and they have three distinct weapon ports that I could see, one on each 'wing' and that menacing nose cannon. As they passed they took my squadron down to just two of us left untouched and one of my Minotaur fighters at about two-thirds maneuverability and a blind spot on its port side.

As the three of us massed together again I pushed us hard forward toward the enemy fighters, hoping they wouldn't expect us to chase them after handing us such a heavy blow. Then, as soon as I saw the reaction from them in accelerating more and changing their direction, I turned hard over and told Cerb "Punch it toward the rest of the fighters." I came out two or three seconds later and we were just crossing into forward motion back toward the Canada. She was a good distance away, but not far enough as I thought about what must be going on with Paulsen and the two bombers I saw evading or barreling through fighters on what appeared to be an intercept course for her. Her. Was it the ship, life's blood to my combat effectiveness, or was it Paulsen I was truly concerned about. It's a fickle and short-lived life as a pilot. If that was the case, why was I just thinking about that now when twenty minutes ago I was more concerned with her diamond flush draw? Hell, I'm not even sure I'll live to see that play out anyway. I'll bet Knisse has a monster hand or something. Maybe pocket 3s or 5s? Hard to believe she'd have stayed. And Lee had said he had a five...dammit, back to biz!

We punched our speed up and shot straight for her. I noticed the other alien bombers slowly approaching us from behind and right up our z axis about twenty degrees and gaining, but not really at an overtake speed. It seemed like they were just going to follow us in? Or maybe they had figured out their advantage and were just observing me now. I suddenly felt alone in the dark, thousands of kilometers away from anyone. Except for aliens intent on killing me. My mind raced through options, but I found no solace in any solutions... I had run through my bag of tricks and had only a handful of weapons left with even less ammo for anything particularly inventive. I wondered if they didn't understand why I led them away and then led them toward the ship? Maybe they were just trying to figure out what this alien group was doing now? Or maybe they've just finally figured it out. That seems more like it. They're taunting me. Playing the cat and mouse game and they don't really need to be sneaky at all when they've got the advantage. Well, in about forty seconds or so they're gonna follow me right into the swarm of our remaining fighters. Let's see how they like that! This one mouse may not be much, but the swarm should take care of them!

***

Damn I hate the feeling that someone knows what I'm thinking. The bombers started a hard acceleration that would overtake me about ten seconds before I even reach the range of any of our fellow fighters. Even then I don't know if they'll be able to help. That's just getting into range, and these beasties have been able to shrug off a lot more than our long range weapons can dish out.

"Cerb, What are our options given the scenario we're in?"

Cerb took more than three seconds just to process that question. NEVER a good thing when it takes a tactical AI that long to think about things. Not that they're always right or even close to flawless in their tactics, but considering the sheer arsenal of knowledge and processing power at his disposal, I shudder to think of the miniscule odds of the 'favorable choice' after that much deliberation.

"Given the scenario and the fact that you didn't really specify what our goals are, I'd recommend we modify our course slightly, as indicated on the nav screen, for a direct intercept with the Canada based on a required ejection of your person from this vessel in approximately in the next ten to twelve point four seconds. That should give you a trajectory that would take you to a higher than eighty percent chance of discovery before you pass through sensor range of the Canada. That doesn't account for other vessels nor the fact that you'd drift toward the Earth should you miss the Canada."

"Jesus Cerb, you're a mountain of hope here..."

"Tactically, sir, the best option for the fleet would be for us to close on the enemy and hope for the slim, eleven point two percent, chance that we would be able to hurt the enemy vessels or severely damage them through fatal collisions with our remaining group. 'Go out in a blaze of glory' I believe is the term, sir."

They were closing faster than anticipated now and Cerb began to have the other fighters wander behind us for cover. We started to vary our course ever-so-slightly ourselves as we decided not to allow some random shot to get us once we came within their range.

I spotted Knisse barreling toward us on an intercept course, with five of her squadron fighters in a slightly larger attack pattern. I took refuge in her opportunity to avenge me, as I noticed we were just falling into enemy range as we understood it. And the warning of energy weapons fire blazed all around me as my sound approximators bellowed klaxons and old-style laser blast sounds to give me a better perception of the battle.

The damaged Minotaur fighter bought it, as it still had a blind spot and limited maneuverability. It just zig'd into some enemy fighter and probably didn't even know it until it exploded. The other Minotaur fighter, one of Lee's heavy-hitters, was starting to get overwhelmed as point defense and deflectors could only do so much, and it was difficult to avoid the excellent targeting of the enemy bombers when we weren't really zigging nor zagging much, really just more running erratically in a straight line. Heh, I have this image of someone waving their arms to avoid getting shot, rather than actually moving.

The last Minotaur stumbled, so to speak, as it must have been hit by something that took out yaw control and some of its speed. As it tumbled away in a slow roll, I noticed that the enemy just let it go and came right up on me. They were close enough to annihilate me if they chose to.

They just continued to close, without firing more than a few shots to remind me they were there. I've never been so angry. And at someone who wouldn't kill me. It made no sense, but I felt cheated of my death in the epic battle. After all, wasn't I enough of an opponent that they needed to kill me? Was I that little of a threat now that they just wanted to taunt me? Or was the chase too exciting for them and they didn't want it to end? "Come on. Do it! Take the shot you cowards!" I found myself yelling at them. I turned to sit facing backward and willed them to attack even as we continued evasive maneuvers. I had a nearly-unobstructed view of them, magnified by the rear optical lenses, and couldn't help but notice how unassuming and menacing they appeared at the same time. Angular, with those hunched-over top-mounted wings and that gaping maw on the front that was the port which constituted their main nose cannon. There were no visible cockpit signs, and the body was blocky and seemed like cast iron but a little slimy. I've probably seen something like it in a movie or a video game as a kid. Funny thing is, that looks more like a turn-of-the-century freighter idea rather than an advanced alien machine kicking our asses all over our own system!

I wonder if Paulsen is aware of my situation? It's soothing to think that someone might actually care that I died here today. Maybe this is that epiphany moment and I'm just in that time-stop where all things become clear? If I lived to tell her, would I? God I wonder what she had in the poker game? It had to be diamonds, right? "Cerb..."

I suddenly ducked reflexively as a swarm of fighters blew right past my magnified screen and smashed into the enemy formation. Two blew into the lead ship in true kamikaze glory, while one bounced off another and two more had independent direct impacts on other alien bombers.  Two others completely missed any of the enemy fighters but had been going so fast it looked like they'd be quite a while before getting back into this fight.

## VI.

*<Hey, mister "I shall be immortal" there? Little hard to be
immortal if you're letting the aliens look right up your skirt, isn't it?>*
Came the comm from Knisse. Her fighter blew past slowing down and
then came into formation with me.

The enemy bombers had scattered and accelerated away from the
chaos of the kamikazes and were suddenly involved in firefights of
their own. I kept pace somewhat with the wreckage of the lead
bomber.

"What the hell was that, Lieutenant? You just destroyed four or five
rearmed and fully operational fighters to save a wounded fighter.
Couldn't you have come up with anything better?" I was grateful, but I
didn't want to seem too enthusiastic to save my ass! I've got a hard-ass
rep to maintain.

"Actually sir, I've restored sensor functionality and we do have our
plasma cannon fully armed and operational. Additionally I've run
some interesting scenarios..."

"Not now, Cerb!" I shut him down quick, before he verbally killed me
from boredom.

*<You're welcome, Ortiz.>* Knisse shot back, laugh and sneer
apparent even to me. *<And don't think dying is going to make me feel
any worse when I collect my winnings after I get back.>*

Ahh, Poker!! "Well, I'm not dead and you don't have the winning
hand, so even if I had died you should feel guilty for taking the pot.
Besides, all I want to know before I die is what you've got that would
make you throw away your money so recklessly? I think the term 'No
card can help you' would be pretty useful for you to think of in this
case." Seriously, there were maybe two hands that could beat me:
pocket threes or pocket fives. And there's no way she had either.
Right?

## Catalino Tolejano, II

<Tell you what, Colonel Ortiz. Before you or I die, I'll let you know what I have. Then you can stop prancing around with your drawers down in front of the aliens trying to get yourself shot up instead of losing gracefully back at the Canada. I can expect the same in return? >

"Done. I know you have ..."

<Hold up.> She shut me down quick. <Look at that...> She trailed off and I started checking equipment. Nothing too crazy going on, although the enemy was actually doing only fairly well against the other fighters. And then I looked over at the alien bomber wreckage still floating along it's last course, not too far from us to eyeball. It had been split into three sections almost, with a huge gash across the starboard side of the fuselage and the port wing basically sheared away from the hull. The wreckage just floated along there, moving in the same direction as we were. And floating in that gash was an alien.

It's hard to explain what it looked like without referencing a mishmash of different things. At first glance, I'd say it looked like a burned table lamp built from bug exoskeleton? I figured it must be burned from some sort of internal explosion or something. It was a greenish-black figure reflecting off the sunlight out here, with various areas that looked like they had decompressed badly from the vacuum. It took a second to catch my breath when another one crawled out onto the hull outside and started to spray it with some sort of hand-held stuff that looked like spray-foam insulation for a house. This one looked like the other, minus the decompression marks.

The creatures had four stubby-looking legs, spread around a more oval shaped body section, which honestly resembled a table with four legs. Well, a fat, chitinous table with four articulated legs that looked like they were a blend between a tarantula and a lizard. On top of the table section was a tall, oval-shaped spire that got wider near the top before descending into what looked like a head dangling on the end of a lengthy neck. There were two arm-type appendages on each side, with the larger arms on top with large hook -type claws at the ends. The smaller, central located arms had what looked like claws, or fingers I suppose, since it was obviously using its long pointy 'fingers' to use the spray-foam gun. The stubby legs moved in a spider-like fashion as it clutched the damaged hull working its way toward the front. When it got to its closest point near the floating body, it actually tried to reach it, but was unsuccessful. I actually felt some empathy toward its dejected form as it slumped, if perhaps only in my mind, as it gave up its vain attempt to recover its comrade. It looked at me. Of course it couldn't see me inside my ship surrounded by the hull, but as it looked at me I got the feeling it was thinking about our lost pilots and fallen comrades in that fleeting moment. And then I felt the familiar ire as I remembered my lost friends and recalled the need to annihilate those that had taken their lives. And this was one of them.

*<Jesus, Colonel. I think it's lookin' at us.>*

It went back to its task and started to climb inside and seal up the gash with the pink sealant. I watched and decided that it's face was some sort of helmet. Maybe it was all a suit, but it seemed very organic. I tried to analyze its image in my head, not even bothering with the playback. After all, I had just glimpsed my first true alien species. Not only was it ugly, but it was kicking my butt all up and down the Mars corridor here. I brought up Cerb's analysis of the enemy fighter and noted that all information, while somewhat incomplete given our lack of knowledge, indicated that this vessel would never be combat-capable. After all, its nose maw was gouged almost in half, with a wing missing and they were using spray-foam to seal it. Odds are looking pretty bad for that ship. And so much the better.

"Knisse. Cerb doesn't think they're gonna get combat-capable. Ever. I've got plenty of video on that thing, and I presume you do too. Let's transmit that to Canada and leave these things. Maybe they die slowly and we relish the cold revenge. Or, maybe they get picked up and when this is all over we just made our first humanitarian gesture of good will. Either way, I've got to get to Canada and get rearmed and a new set of drawers before I'm much good to anyone. Coming along or you gonna stay out here and check on the other kids in the playground?"

*<Hell, I haven't even fired a shot and I've already got two more kills than you do. I better stay out here where the big kids play while you run back to your crib, mister immortal. Just don't go cheating and looking at my cards. I'd hate to hear how you couldn't get back in the fight because you were too busy crying down in the Mess over your*

**87**

*loss at cards.>* With that she bolted away at an ugly angle yelling "Yeeee Hawwww" for probably thirty seconds, I swear.

I could have comm'd her again to continue our conversation, but I knew she was getting in the zone and I didn't need to screw that up for her. I'd already lost most of the table, no need to push anyone else' luck. Plus, when her other two fighters caught back up with her she'd be a sight for sore eyes to any of the remaining fighter jocks out here.

I watched the alien bomber for a few more seconds, alone this time. I wasn't sure if I felt good about leaving them out here, when I could just kill them. I thought about the situation if it were reversed and I'd want some honor on the battlefield, but I don't know if they even understand that. At least I will know that they have to go back and tell their buddies that they got beat by us. I wonder if they hold grudges.

"You should look at this, sir!" Came Cerb's voice in the cockpit. He brought up a tactical overlay on the three-dimensional display around me and started running projections. Poker winners, like in Chess, win with long-term strategy not just luck or timing. Those things help, but getting lucky doesn't make you good. Cerb is good. He's far better at long-term strategic analysis than I am so I just floated for a little bit as we headed toward the Canada, listening while he played out his conclusions. The only thing that AIs really lacked when it came to strategy was the gut instinct or feel for the playing field. AIs didn't observe nor plan for panic nor irrational behavior. It has no place in their scenarios. It's understandable that AIs, because erratic or unpredictable behavior can't be analyzed to a conclusion, ignore crazy decisions. It also means, though, that they spend a lot of time analyzing the reasonable options!

"So, you're saying that the alien bombers are following a decidedly random pattern logically descending upon us like a countdown which should end once we reach Canada, thus they'll not only get us but have a chance at the Canada? Why not just take us out now and get the Canada later? Or vice versa?"

"There are several options, but the most logical is that the efficient option is to get us all together. If they wait just a few seconds longer while we enter the carrier, then they could just blow us up inside. However, given their timing, and the fact that they continue to adjust based on us, indicates that they are either perplexed by us specifically or they are using us as the base timer so we are the key."

"So, if we just stop here will they stop with us? Or if we change course will they follow us toward the other capital vessels where we can get them in a crossfire?"

"Actually, we don't have enough information to be sure. If we choose one of those actions, I could then answer the question. And that would give us some intel into their motives. Presuming that I am correct about these hypotheses. There is always the possibility of a course of action that doesn't follow logical prediction." That last line is the AI way of saying 'There are plenty of other crazy, illogical human ideas that come up often enough that I have to account for but cannot predict.'

It had been a while out here running around with the bombers, and I hadn't really taken the precious seconds to find out where the battle was as a whole. "How's the WC's BG doing, Cerb?" It was obvious to Cerb, I assume, that I was going to ask that. As I asked the data was already appearing on the overlay and it gave me that creepy feeling that things were reading my mind. I hate that feeling. I wonder if I have some 'tells' in poker that I haven't been able to remove? Hmmm... don't feel like it, but I lose my share of money too, so who knows? Now's not really the time.

I spent extremely precious seconds reviewing the data. Unfortunately and fortunately it doesn't take long to see that the Winston Churchill is about to become the only surviving member of its Battle Group. And worse, it doesn't look like she's going to last too much longer if she continues on a direct course toward that behemoth Alien mother ship! There were several fighters working in concert around her, keeping a few alien bombers and anti-ship weapons from getting to her, but she was still going toe-to-toe with an alien monstrosity having lost her important cover vessels which could at least have helped protect each other with CPD (Concentrated Point Defense) in order to really make an impression in the aliens. Not that she wasn't doing well enough, but even with fighters from Canada and the arsenal at her disposal, it seemed bleak hoping that she'd make enough of a problem for that monster ship. It had already demonstrated devastating firepower, and I doubted that at point-blank range all it had were the weapons we'd already seen!

"Cerb, head toward the Winston Churchill at max accel and we'll use her as cover, then make a strafing run against the alien mother ship. We're obviously not going to do too much to that ship, but if it distracts them from the WC then we've done our part to buy her some additional time. And monitor the aliens stalking us and let me know how they react to our course and tactic changes. We'll head for Canada after the strafing run and get rearmed and repaired, if possible, before this fight ends."

Combat in space is quiet. There are no external sounds other than the ones we 'make' internally, and artificially I might add, with our sound approximators. Worse, possibly, than that is the fact that space is vast and empty. I was actually going to have about ninety-eight seconds before I had any bombers in range given their current locations and trajectories, with another forty until I was within the weapons envelope to even help the WC or even start that run on the Alien Mother Ship.  So, I took some time to ravage down some much-needed food and water, while making sure to relieve myself before my system got all out of whack from 'holding it' if you know what I mean. It's not glorious nor sexy, but it's a necessity of this life and not all that interesting to the glory-hounds who usually tell our stories. But sometimes, those comforts remind us of life and just how nice the little things can be!

About the time I hit the threat envelope for the first bomber, which was itself conveniently headed toward the WC as well, I watched it abruptly whip over into an odd and unnecessary maneuver taking it on a trajectory right away from the WC. Good, that brings it closer to me and away from them! I adjusted my heading to take me a little further away from the bomber,  as if I had dismissed him and was heading right for the Winston Churchill now. And then it veered away at a steep angle, directly toward the Canada. An suddenly so did most of the bombers, whether or not they were tied up with fighters between the Carrier and the battle at the AV1! Their abrupt change in course seemed to confuse many of our young pilots, and the fact of their great speed advantage got them out of real danger from the fighters rather quickly. The cheers over the radio by many of the rookies indicated that they felt the bombers were disengaging and running, but I knew that they were all about to take out our home- obvious when you saw all their trajectories converging on the Canada. And they had a lead with faster acceleration and speeds already. Many pilots took to the tail of the bombers and tried to chase them down, but the faster and more agile bombers did a good job of either dodging shots or minimizing hits into superfluous strikes.

***

I fired a direct comm to Paulsen while Cerb gave an automatic update to the Tactical officer on the Canada that they were coming. "Paulsen. Ortiz. You've got eight, correction nine, inbound bombers moving faster than any of us can get to them." Damn them, they let us engage them all out here in the middle and probably had their pick of going after the WC or the Canada once were were all wound up here. They'll have probably thirty seconds of alone-time with Canada before the bulk of the pursuing fighters reach them. Damn!"You'll have minimal support as it looks like Clark and Carter will be the first wings in at about twelve seconds after they enter weapons range. I'm about thirty-four seconds out from that, but by myself in this shape, I'm not really going to do more than annoy them."

<Ortiz. Paulsen. Copy that and thanks for the intel. I think we can handle them until the fighters get here, but not for long if you can't get them off our back. I'll have Cerb start downloading his AI matrix update into a new fighter for your new orders. As you know, it's not the hardware we're lacking now but the pilots. I've got an X-4, designate Valkyrie 2 Command, along with two other dumb fighters ready on the pad. I just need to get someone into it. Tactical has been working with the ground crew directly to get the two support birds loaded with Gauss cannons and as much ammo as they can carry. After they burn through that they'll just have their single plasma cannons. Valkyrie 2 we've loaded with two plasma pulse cannons, a Gauss cannon with normal ammo, and mounted some extra shield emitters to make it more survivable against the bombers. For external ordnance we took most for point defense and added in four of our Xavier capital missiles. Your mission will be to proceed at best possible speed toward the Alien Main Vessel, AV1, with minimal

*enemy engagement, and proceed to take her out. If you are able to harass her enough, you should also draw off some of those bombers and give us a break. As well, you may keep the WC around longer and that increases likelihood of a victory. I won't lie to you, Javier, it's a suck op that will bring down Hell upon you in the best-case scenario. If you're not successful, there really won't be much to do except harass them until we're all dead. So, no pressure, eh?>*

"Just tell me where she is and I'll be there."

*<You'll be doing a combat hop, assuming you're wearing your suit. Valkyrie 2 is in Bay 2, slot 13, with her support vessels in 3 and 19. Every slot around 13 is empty, so you can park your fighter anywhere you want. Just get your cute ass into that fighter and go get some alien hearts for me. I need to add some to my collection.>*

"You always did have a way with words, Ezera. Just keep your head on straight and safe and I'll make sure to make staying alive worth your while. Bay 2 slot 13 confirmed. I'll be there in forty-one seconds from mark. Any chance you can turn the light on for me, honey?"

*<You know, Ortiz, I've always felt we were made for each other. Maybe it's...>* I lost comms as the alien bombers entered weapons range and either jammed the signals or just took out her comm towers. Either way, this crap was getting old really fast. I checked Cerb's upload and it looked like it was still happening, so I was pretty sure that Canada lost the comm tower. With Cerb updating to the Canada at max speed, he wasn't really doing too much for me right now. And not much for the next eight seconds it looks like. I pulled up the Canada's tactical schematic and watched as the bombers entered range and started lengthy assault runs across several angles across most sides of her. Her defense drones were out, point-defense pods were bursting almost constantly, and she was rolling to present lower profiles at the stronger enemy concentrations. And she was still taking damage in several sections as the bombers were unrelenting in their ability to fire all three plasma cannons and shrug off salvos of defensive fire.

## VII.

The Canada started to slow her spin and I verified that it would bring bay 2 right into my path upon my arrival. It also meant I was going to be coming in really hot and have to drop in backwards as I slowed down. Damn, this was getting worse and worse. I flipped the fighter over as I got close to the right time to begin slowing down and then waited one second longer than I should have. It occurred to me that I needed to come in hot enough that I don't have to dodge anyone otherwise I'll never get in there. It's already going to be hard enough to get into that rotating bay at combat speeds. Like I need more challenges today?

I really should find out if there is some sort of telepathic broadcaster in my head. Or if I owe the great god Murphy some sort of penance for past sins or something? On the opposite side, Canada got a good swat at a bomber and sent it into an uncontrolled thrust. Which then took it right into the opening doors of bay 2 where it appeared to explode on impact, taking the power and door control offline. I cut into hard deceleration and managed to stay conscious this time. I watched as several fighters, Knisse included, swarmed onto the bombers around Canada and started to actually make some headway.

Six of the remaining bombers switched into anti-fighter maneuvering and started to re-take the advantage in combat as they were less sitting ducks now. One of them finally fell under enough firepower to turn it into Swiss cheese as more of the centaur-bug aliens were ejected from the internal chambers. One of them had some sort of hand-held weapon it fired at nearby fighters as it floated off into oblivion. If I had the time, I'd think about what that means philosophically.

Instead, I slowed down enough but still rendezvoused with the hanger doors of the Canada. At the last possible moment, I flipped over and used the nose to gently wedge my fighter into the opening of the doors. I had actually thought I'd be able to fit between the doors, but apparently I still struggle with math and got her caught a good half-meter away from the widest section. I blew the external and internal hatches and started to pop out of my fighter for my space-walk, or space-run I suppose really, toward the honeycomb of fighter bays and get myself into Valkyrie 2. Assuming I didn't get shot nor screw this up worse.

My short-range radio communication came on. *<Nice damned landing, Colonel. Remind me to never let you drive me anywhere after this. With flying skills like that, maybe I should give you a shuttle and get a real pilot into Valkyrie 2?>*

"Hey, it's not any worse than your historic and mind-numbing landing at Edinburgh when we weren't even IN combat?!"

*<No fair! I told you that was an instrumentation issue. You know the CN440 was prone to issues with its 3D ILS system at civilian airstrips, especially outside North America.>*

"Paulsen, you were drunk! We both were. Whatever the reason, you missed a three kilometer runway!" I hope she could hear the humor in my voice. If not, she was gonna come down here and shoot me before I got in that fighter! I cleared the external hatch, clipped myself to the handle, then made sure my suits minimal thrusters worked. I shouldn't need them, but when you do isn't the time to check! They checked good and I switched on the grav boots at about 40% so that I could move quickly. As I unlatched myself I noticed my shadow brightly on the hull. I turned to look and saw what must have been a plasma pulse being deflected by a drone that was sitting above my position. Beyond that there was an alien bomber growing larger and firing multiple plasma blasts that were starting to overload the drone's defensive capabilities. It did light things up for me as we spun into the shadow side of the ship rotation. I think that thing was shooting at me...

*<You're welcome, jerk.>*

"Paulsen, I swear I owe you a kiss and a drink when we get outta this!"

*<Come back in one piece and I'll give you more than the kiss. Now, get your ass in that bird while I try to come up with a solution to the*

*door problem.*> Plasma lit up the darkness around me as some shots started to make it past. I felt like I was in some sort of action vid as I sprinted toward the opening with bright bolts of light raining down onto the hull of my fighter and then the doors as I leaped through the opening. I was barely meters inside when the fighter exploded behind me. I know this because the last thing I saw was a super-bright light and the nose hurtling past my legs toward the fighter bay honeycombs.

***

Paulsen was tapping my head. I turned over, drool separating from face and pillow, to see her presumably naked form wrapped in the tussled sheets with me. She smelled like lilies and looked disheveled enough for me to understand how well our night had gone. As my vision started to take in the bright sunlight permeating every surface of the room, I started to recognize this room. Was this Edinburgh, that little place called Thelma Noir we were in? She's beautiful and smiling at me with those dimples that match. Never mind. I've been here with her before. What was I just doing. It was something important. You know, one of those dreams where you were dreaming of glory and saving the world but lost it when you awoke? The feelings of unfulfilled destiny and depression that you weren't going to save everyone still lingering. But you can't remember what you were actually doing, no matter how hard you try. It feels awful for a few minutes, like you've just let down the World. And here you are with those feelings, looking at a beautiful woman, who is speaking to you but you don't actually hear anything because you're too caught up in the dream.

"Come on, sleepyhead!" She was speaking so softly it was almost like a lullaby. "You can't just lie around all day. You've got work to do."

I glanced at the clock. It was Fourteen-twenty. I felt terrible as my body senses started to come back to me. My neck was sore, my back was killing me, and my leg felt like I had thrown out my knee again. "Jesus, Ez, I feel like you really beat the crap out of me. Maybe we should take it a little easy tonight, otherwise sex with you is gonna kill me! Not that I'm complaining! I just need to be able to walk is all, okay?" She started talking again but I couldn't hear her. I saw the lips moving but the ears just didn't get anything. "Ez, hold on a sec. Did you scream in my ears again? I can't hear a damned thing! Oh man I've got a hangover." My head throbbed as I sat up. "We didn't get in another fight last night, did we? I didn't just blame sex for some sort of brawl injury did I? Damn it feels like I lost, whatever it was."

She sat straight up in the bed. She was definitely naked. She always did have the best breasts I'd ever seen. And she was my age and that was still the case. The pain washed away for the moment. "You are the most beautiful woman," I told her in my most suave morning-haven't-had-any-coffee-and-probably have-terrible-morning-breath voice.. "There's nothing I can think of better than waking up next to your naked beauty every day."

She stopped talking and just stared at me, her almond eyes squeezing ever-so-slightly as she thought about it. "Then why are you wearing your combat suit?" She asked.

"What?" I looked down and I was wearing a pilot's combat suit. And my leg was suddenly bleeding out onto the sheets and pooling in the most peculiar forms. She dipped a finger in the blood, sucked on it with an erotic grin, then punched me across the jaw knocking me out of the bed. I cried out like a girl as the pain in my leg and the rest of my body came back to me. I landed on the wall opposite the bed and just hung there in midair like a marionette on strings. She got out of bed and approached me. She really was beautiful. And naked.

"Javier, you are one twisted son of a bitch. If you're just laying around down there having wet dreams about me, I'm gonna come down there and kill you myself if you don't get your ass and that fighter group off my ship! You hear me? Now get your act together and maybe do something for humanity and not just your libido! You hear me Colonel Ortiz? Javier?"

She kissed me with a full press of her body as the sunlight blinded me and I found myself in a chaotic cargo bay. Wait, it wasn't a cargo bay, I was just looking at the ceiling from a wall. I was in a flight suit, full rig, with my feet planted on the wall as I stood sideways at some ridiculous angle.

"Damn! This doesn't bode well...."

## Last Man Dying

***

Warning bells were going off in my helmet while my heads-up display showed a suit decompression countdown and several points of damage to the suit. Apparently the back padding and support structure had taken a lot of damage. My leg was killing me and I saw blood spheres slowly floating away toward a cratered doorway into this chamber. There was a blood mark on the fighter honeycomb structure that was perhaps made by my leg? I was still quite fuzzy on how I put a blood impression over there but ended up fifty meters over here on a side wall. I pulled off some of the repair straps that just sit on the outside of the suit like slap-patches for just this kind of thing. Since the suit is custom-fit to your body, it's not hard to repair any leaks or damage with what amount to suit band-aids. I just have to give it a little electrical charge when in place to get the adhesive to activate and bond with the suit. "The blood won't matter" - that's what the egg-heads tell us. As the first to really test that theory in practice on these suits, it's lucky for me that they're right!

After taking a few seconds to patch my suit and assess my location, which means try to figure out what the hell is going on, things start to come back to me. I was outside the Canada getting out of my fighter, I recalled. I had parked it *IN* the doors and had needed to get inside. What fighter was I looking for?

Suddenly three fighters sidled out of the honeycomb and dropped into a line to get out the door. Looks like the hole in the door was big enough for them to get through. One of the fighters, an ugly-looking X-4 with a bunch of extra ordnance jury rigged on the outside and just the command module entry light on slid sideways toward me maneuvering like it was going to hit me. I started to walk backwards up the wall as it dropped, so it wouldn't hit me. Then I saw the marking on the module. *Valkyrie 2: Mjr Ezera Paulsen.* Hey, that's the fighter I need!

"Sir, if you're not too busy, your chariot awaits. Major Paulsen asked me to come get you before you said or did anything more stupid. Once you're in and we're under way, your comms will be restored. Do you understand me, sir?" Cerb sounded like a tired old butler who was sick of catering to petulant children. It might be the difference in his voice sound from this ship. In a normal scenario, I'd have his voice and all working for me, but now that I recalled what was going on I remember that he was doing an emergency dump and probably didn't take the time to get everything quite right. For the AI this was probably efficient enough.

I released the grav boots and floated over the few meters to the entry and slid in. As the hatches sealed behind me I sat down in the command module and nearly knocked myself out again as the indescribable pain of my back touching anything shot through me. Good thing my comms were off, cuz there was that scream again.

"Cerb, get us out that hole and headed toward AV1. Have you been briefed on the mission?"

"Sir, while your greatness slumbered I was working. For the record, I anticipated your decision and named our support wing Achilles one and two. Please confirm that resonates well with you."

"Conf..."

"Also, I'm going to administer some meds with the onboard system to help with the pain and see if I can get the bots to do something for the back of your suit. Major Paulsen would like to speak with you on secure channel 123.7 when you're able."

"Confirmed on Achilles one and two. Get us moving at best possible speed. Paulsen can wait a few moments while I get up to speed myself. What happened to me in the hangar? How long was I out? Why did she cut off my comms? And what's the status of the Winston Churchill as far as its ability to support us or vice versa? Go!" I took a look at the hole and the Canada's hull as we cleared the ship. Cerb already had my favorite tactical setup with full view running before we got to the doors.

"Already taking the best course to make time and avoid delays, sir. You were caught in the blast from your exploding fighter and accelerated into the hangar honeycomb then bounced over toward the wall where your grav boots conveniently caught and held you in place. Shrapnel from the fighter tore up your leg and suit, along with the damage to your back and the suit's back. You were unconscious for eighty-seven seconds and then began babbling about drunken landings and naked majors for thirty-eight more seconds. I think it's obvious why she cut off your comms. Winston Churchill has taken a decidedly defensive stance off the stern of the enemy vessel AV1, outside of main weapons range, where it is currently working damage control and adequately defending itself from the minimal weapons firing on it."

I noticed how badly chewed up the hangar doors and the area inside the hangar bay were. A lot of it appeared to be from hits by the bomber that was chasing me, I think. Some of it no-doubt from my exploding fighter. Either way, this bay wasn't going to do anyone any good. It's unfortunate that we probably won't need it anyway. Probably won't even need one full bay for the fighters that make it back, if any do.

# VIII.

We shot away from the Canada so fast I was out for a few more seconds, or at least I don't recall those seconds. Probably not good for someone as beat up, physically and mentally, as I was. As I came back I started to get a read on the tactical situation. Fighters were swarming around the three remaining bombers I found on my tac screen, but I couldn't get a read on the Canada herself.

"Cerb, why can't I get a read on the Canada?" She's obviously still there, since we just left her. I see the three bombers and the fighters on them, I see the Canada of course, but I can't get any damage readouts nor assessment data?" There was a destroyer on the other side of her, acting as her last defender since the other vessels had already fallen to alien fire.

"Sorry sir. The Canada hasn't restored main systems and has several power and system-wide issues all over the vessel. Once they restore main systems, assuming they get the chance, they'll get combat data and transmissions back on line. Right now, all they've got are the personal nets and the individual command posts around the ship since the bridge went down. You should really talk with Major Paulsen on channel 123.7 sir. She can give you the most up-to-date data on what they're going to do. I don't really speculate well."

Damn! I already forgot to comm her. I set it up and noticed the irony that the meds Cerb had administered were kicking in as she came on. "Paulsen, Ortiz. What's the sit-rep on the Canada. I can stay and help with those last few bombers before running off after AV1." I knew she was going to object, but I had to at least offer to help them.

<*You turn that ship around and I'll fire on you myself, Ortiz!*> She didn't sound too great. Not like she was in pain, but she had a gritty sound to her voice like she had been sucking in dirt before getting on the comm with me.

"Understood. How are you personally, then?" We were on a secure individual personal comm net. If I was going to ask, now would be a good time.

*<I'm just fine, Ortiz. How are you? Nice weather we're having out here at Mars, eh? You see the game last night? Dolphins really annihilated the Chargers, eh? You hear tonight's forecast? Slightly cloudy with a chance of getting your ass blown up by freaking aliens while an idiot asks how I'm doing!>*

"I ask because it's important to me. For me to do this and do it well, I would feel better knowing that you're okay. Besides, I was dreaming about you and that actually means something to me. Plus... I really wanna know if you had the diamond draw I put you on. I know it was diamonds. I think Knisse had two pair or maybe a straight draw with ace/four or something. Tell me before I die. Put my mind at ease?" I really did want to know about her poker hand. Plus, asking about that put some brakes on the first part in case I was too heavy for the moment. She could just drive past that and hit me on the poker front instead.

*<Jesus Ortiz. You really are an idiot. We lost the Mess early on when one of the bombers kamikazed the port bow and took the Mess out along with most of the section. By the way, you'll need to find new quarters. Yours are somewhere near Jupiter by now, I think. Don't even dream about suggesting it.>*

"Well, speaking of dreams. I WAS just dreaming about it. Edinburgh. It's not like you to be so shy!"

*<Yeah, everyone heard your dream about Edinburgh. Thanks for that. You make it through this and I'll consider letting you bunk with me until other accommodations are made for you. Just get yourself back here in one piece. I gotta go before someone else starts dreaming about me. Now, go kick some ass and get me those hearts. Ciao!>*

"See you when I get back. Now that I have something, somewhere, to live for!" I said it as dramatically as I could. I couldn't help with the humor at a time like this. This was a seriously effing (I tried to quit swearing ages ago, maybe time again) mission. My three fighters against the Alien gargantuan menace while my carrier was being gutted by the enemy. Great! Now I really feel heroic about this.

I shall be immortal.

# *Catalino Tolejano, II*

\*\*\*

Cerb took us on an elliptical course that would avoid the bombers between us and our target: AV1. I barely kept from engaging in a few of the dogfights which practically spilled right into our path. I hated slipping by while my comrades were dying, but I knew what orders were and what I needed to do for the "big picture" of things. Still didn't feel any less slimy. And it's not like no one knew I was there. They were all just too busy to do anything about it. None of the fighters I passed comm'd me. Either they had an inkling of what I was doing or just didn't have the time. I'm gonna hope it's the first reason.

We stayed in a tight formation and slowed ourselves into extreme weapons range on the port side of the nose of AV1. I expected incoming fire but received none. Not even the "warning" of targeting beams to tell me they knew I was there. Maybe they already detected I didn't have anything good at long range? Maybe they were out of ordnance? Yeah right. It must be something else. I took a look at the Winston Churchill and could easily tell that she wasn't doing so well. Clearly some of the munitions from AV1 had been getting through, as I found several sections that appeared to be open to space, several oxygen fires, and an assortment of debris fields all around her bow as she continued to defend against a dozen capital missiles in each salvo from the alien ship. I passed a serene cemetery of debris from of one of the WC's screening destroyers, maybe the Shiva that had been sent by the Canada. We dodged several large pieces, using them as cover once we felt that we could traverse them successfully.

Two bombers dropped out of the Alien behemoth and headed directly toward us. They accelerated quickly and moved on an obvious direct intercept course. Under normal circumstances, I'd say the odds were stacked in their favor even though we had the numerical advantage. I thought about running them toward the WC, but she was already dealing with enough. At least now since the proverbial cat was out, it meant we didn't need to appear to have any ulterior motives either. We quickly closed on the two bombers. As we approached, Cerb updated our data calling them Gunships Alpha and Bravo. I looked at the readings, as he explained his schematic, and found that these were probably some sort of defender or specialized duo of bombers. They had smaller apertures for their cannons, indicating smaller striking power. However, they had several and appeared to have a variety of defensive adaptations which would take more firepower to saturate. We closed on them in three... two... They opened fire with their smaller weapons, covering a far greater area for multiple smaller impacts. All three of the fighters took damage, but it was minimal. It looked now like these were defensive vessels and were just going to whittle us down until they could do some real damage. Or worse, they were going to make us waste our offensive ordnance on their far less significant vessels. In either case, they had to be removed from our path. We concentrated fire on Alpha, as we moved in and out of our moderate range. We stuck to plasma cannons since we weren't going to waste ammunition on these defenders. One thing was certain, there was no way I was going to get these warheads near AV1 until the defenders were out of the picture. And even then, I would need to practically land on AV1 to make sure these elephantine missiles didn't get destroyed by point-defense.

Valkyrie 2 moved like a hippo, though, as I tried to maneuver for decent firing solutions. Even Cerb didn't like maneuvering her, which he made clear in colorful phrases I never expected to hear from an AI. As our dance with the defender bombers moved us closer to the giant ship, we finally started to make a dent in Alpha's absorption rate and began to dissect her into composite parts. It took precious time though, of which we ran out as Bravo came to his brother's aid by flipping over and making a run straight for us. We got him with several direct hits as he screened Alpha, but they did little and we were forced to evade. I took after Alpha and sent both my Achilles after Beta with Cerb in control.

\*\*\*

Alpha was still licking his wounds as I moved in for the kill when Cerb updated me that several bombers were in-bound and coming fast. And absolutely coming for us. I continued to chase Alpha along the lengthy horizon of AV1, as the defender chose to use its mother ship's defensive fire as more cover. I checked the number of inbound bombers and glanced at the Canada readout. The Canada still wasn't transmitting, but even the video feed started to show that she was a battered husk of a ship right now. Systems all over were down. She looked burned out all along the hull where Bay 2 had been, no thanks to me. I still saw what constituted defensive fire from several drones and even some manned stations, but with only two bombers around her I felt good that she might hold her own defensively... and then I saw it. Her Nova buoy shot away toward Earth, the recorded system of knowledge which not only gathered all her observations but collected all the data input by the research, tactical, analytical, and whatever other egghead teams you could think of. Bay 2 broke away first, the fracture across the support pylons leaking atmosphere, repair crews, and anything else into the space around it. Then the explosions along the tear started and I caught a few escape pods, shuttles, and fighters hustle away at maximum speed. The two bombers moved in for the kill and unloaded devastation across the tear, with only minimal defensive fire or drones to stop any of it. I hope the aliens died in agony, boiled in their tin cans as they were engulfed in the explosion that blew the Canada apart. A silent bubble of energy, dissolving oxygen fires, and plasma energy rapidly rose in a sphere around the breach, then collapsed on itself and exploded in a brilliant ball of changing colors – like a star being born and dying in a matter of seconds.

I watched calmly, no emotion even though I was alone if I wanted to react. I tried to comm Paulsen directly but got nothing. Not surprising since the EMP from that blast would have knocked out comms anyway around the ship. I knew she was dead. I didn't believe it, couldn't really believe it, but somewhere in the back of my mind I felt it. A peace or serenity I didn't expect. Overwhelmed by guilt that gave everything a weight that was thick and pliable in my mind. Like dancing in hip-level mud.

I thought about the last time I saw her in person, not just in my recent dreams. She had sat across the oval table from me, three from my left and four to my right. She was wearing her black uniform with its green trim. The dark colors of the uniform complimented her smooth, light skin and dark hair like she had been made to make the uniform look good. Her jacket was open to her red undershirt which was form-fitting and padded slightly for impact resistance. She was never good at truly letting her guard down. It was obvious as she protected her cards, even after Thompson and Lee folded. She had been eying the five and three of diamonds, ignoring the king of hearts that accompanied them on the Flop. When the turn (or fourth street) came with the king of spades, she was calm and really didn't give anything away, which is why I was sure she'd had the diamonds. It was just Knisse, Paulsen and I then. I looked over to Knisse and she was grinning like the Cheshire Cat. Now that was dangerous. I looked back to Paulsen and we made eye contact. She winked at me and looked to Knisse waiting for her to bet or check in first position. Paulsen's hair swept over her face, and then the image was gone.

I was looking at the space around me. It was beautiful and silent. I turned to my right and looked at the ominous form of the Alien Main Vessel. It was truly gargantuan and hideously alien even though it didn't really appear too different from something which could have been made on Earth. Hidden within its silhouette I found the Alpha gunship lurking, slowly stalking directly toward me, perhaps hoping it has successfully camouflaged itself in the background of AV1? I would hope that aliens knew there wasn't anything like real stealth out here. After all, they were the ones who traveled across the galaxy or from wherever to us. I incredulously watched him move toward me and just kept floating along, keeping my course and speed the same, headed slowly toward the bow of AV1. He closed so quickly I almost wasn't ready as he passed from extreme to medium range in nearly an instant. He didn't fire right away. As he passed into close range, for him, he opened up with everything he had which probably would have killed me had I been sitting where I should have been. Unfortunately for him, I had read his mind this time. I slammed on acceleration while turning the nose in, which slid the whole ship out to the side but got my nose lined up on him as I swung to his right and toward him, changing the angles. As I lined up on him I fired both my plasma cannons in differing pulse rates right into his nose. If they didn't damage him the light show HAD to have obscured his vision enough to explain why he jerked hard into a 'climb' if you think of us having been on an even plane. It pulled his nose up which cleared the sensors but presented the ship's belly to me and I took off toward it in a pristine attack angle looking down at its exposed underside. As I wailed on it with phased plasma and tried to either burn out its fuselage or my cannons, it spun on its axis to get that side away from me. Not caring, I continued to now fire at its top roof section with agonizing repeated strikes dead center. And then a collision and fire warning came and Cerb jerked the ship hard to port, making my back and ribs ache in sharp, reverberating pain in spite of my meds. The good thing was that we moved to avoid the hail of Gauss projectiles and plasma fire that preceded the two Achilles fighters almost through the Alpha gunship's location in space. Luckily for them, as they split around Alpha the ship didn't explode, but only seemed to die with no power nor any emissions that I could detect.

Apparently Cerb had fared better with the Bravo gunship, as he had marked the locations of the pieces that used to constitute the ship. Damned showoff. I figured that thing must be out of bombers or defenders if it wasn't sending anything else.

I shall be immortal.

## IX.

I had another of my crazy ideas and this one, again, I thought might actually work! I maneuvered right up in front of the Alpha gunship husk and used my ship to slow it down. I checked for the Alien bombers that were inbound and found I had about ten seconds to get this going. Doubtful I'd make it, I decided to start pushing it with the nose of my ship toward AV1. We accelerated hard and Cerb helped keep it in front of us. Achilles wing formed up behind me, as Cerb knew what I was doing. I was going to use the Alpha gunship to screen me from alien fire, and waltz right up to AV1 and unload fiery death right on her doorstep. Had I the time or mental fortitude at this late hour, I might have come up with something else, but it was the best I had and would either be recorded as a brilliant tactic or a warning to avoid plans born of lunacy. Time to find out which.

The bombers were coming up fast on my tail and three sides of me for good measure. "How ironic" I thought, as they were also timed to hit me all within a few seconds of one another. How thoughtful of them to suddenly show a little concern.

Cerb started rotating the Achilles fighters into defensive screening positions around me in a little dance across my rear vertical plane as I hugged the shadow of the bomber and could see AV1 start its barrage of defensive fire, wreaking all sorts of havoc on the bomber, but not enough to saturate my defenses.

<*Hey, mister "I shall be immortal" - you gonna invite anyone else to your party?*> came Knisse's voice over the comm. She was close enough for a tight laser transmission and apparently trailing one of the bomber groups that was closing on me. Her fighter looked like it had been the star target of marksmanship drills and that was just from what I could see with optical sensors!

"Nice of you to join us, Lieutenant. Looks like you're going to be fashionably late but perhaps just in time for the fireworks. Any chance you can take out any of your playmates?"

<*Actually, all I've got left is ramming speed and some seriously bad breath. Any chance you could get any close enough for that?*> She laughed the kind of needed, hearty, and yet still pathetic laugh of someone who knew she'd been beaten and had not much left to give.

"I'll ask them to give a girl a chance, Knisse. Never hurts to ask." I wanted to get her poker hand, now that I was making my suicide run, but I decided to give her a few moments of respectful silence. She was putting her courage together and didn't need me chatting her out of her decision. "Cerb, how does it look for us to make it through the defensive fire to get close enough for a guaranteed strike with all four Xaviers?"

"Given the size and angles presented to AV1, offset by your penchant for absurdly survivable decisions, and the fact that the bombers will have us in range for more than ten seconds et cetera, I give us a strong nine point four percent chance. That's higher than other maneuvers you've done in the last two years and look at us now!"

Nine point four? Wow, I was expecting maybe point four. I suddenly felt good about my odds!

We started to take heavy fire from AV1 as we moved toward her port bow in the lower section, with more of our vessel exposed to the area above us. We kept our low profile so the length of her didn't have a good shot, but that didn't mean she couldn't pummel us from above fairly well. My Achilles fighters, I think I'll call them Helter and Skelter for what it's worth, flipped over and started firing toward the bombers that were moving in. Cerb moved us around behind the gunship husk to be a slightly less-favorable target while I ran through another weapons check to make sure we were ready to deploy.

"Cerb. Command order. If a stray shot kills or renders me unconscious or ineffective at finishing this attack run (you have to be careful with Ais) then you are ordered to proceed toward AV1, releasing the Xaviers at point blank range and then retreat to a safe distance and await further orders. If no orders come, you are ordered to continue to harass the enemy until you are destroyed or rendered ineffective. At that point, return to Earth. Confirm."

"Command orders confirmed. Now, would you let me get back to work? This keeping your ass alive stuff is a constant struggle and quite vexing." Somehow Cerb always knew what to say to me.

"Vexing? Please tell me you didn't just use the word vexing. Remind me later to have you remove that word from your vocabulary."

***

Helter and Skelter kept the bombers off but eventually became barely effective at doing more than intercepting incoming fire, having spent their Gauss and other munitions. Plasma weapons were very difficult to target as the fighters were jostling around so much while the bombers hung out at range and just fired down on us.

Suddenly a storm of plasma and laser fire erupted around the gunship carcass, which kept me safe enough directly behind it, but the concentration of fire overcame the Achilles fighters' point defense, reducing them to heated metal wiffle balls falling away behind me. "Evasive maneuvers but don't bring us into that fire, Cerb" I yelled as I started to look for other avenues into or away from this death-trap. The bombers turned back inward, closing the gap on me suddenly as deadly fire from an angle above us started to rain down while the bombers came in from behind. We had to maneuver below and behind the bomber hull to avoid the majority of fire from in front and above us, basically pinning us into a position behind the bomber carcass until the other bombers could come in and finish the job. I was so caught up in the acrobatics of minimizing the incoming fire, that I hadn't noticed that the huge battleship Winston Churchill had closed on our position firing her own salvos into the side of AV1 as the majority of her fire was concentrated on us! The WC slowed overhead and in front of us, shielding us from the upper and forward annihilation raining down from AV1. Now we just had the bombers behind us to worry about, and the WC had started firing on the bombers from that side of the battered vessel. Cerb jumped us to the other side of the gunship husk so that it was behind us as we continued to close on AV1, with the carcass shield behind us and the WC screening us for most of our remaining travel toward AV1.

*<Ortiz.>* A wet cough echoed through the comm, followed by *<Nutomo here. We're banged up real bad and won't be moving from this spot until we can get some helm control and regain thrust controls. Most of our heavy weapons are out and we've got minimal attitude and rudder control. We've already expended our missile and ammunition stores, so we're going to do our best at covering you for your run.>* WC suddenly unleashed its own hail of plasma and laser fire at the approaching bombers which fell into chaos as they were hit or forced to evade the far more powerful capital weapons. *<If we'd had the control and power, we might have rammed this ship ten minutes ago. Don't worry about us taking a beating, we're just glad we get to help deliver some more pain to these bastards. Good hunting, soldier! Nutomo out.>*

I couldn't see it, but my sensors, which were now tied to the WC being so close that we could almost touch as far as space distances go, showed that she was taking a hail of fire from the forward section of that ship. We came out from under her and quickly dropped below and behind the shielding gunship husk again, right before a barrage of defensive fire from point-blank range slammed into the gunship remains. Debris from the two large vessels was scattering in several directions and even helped to intercept some of the fire as lasers struck space-debris before reaching us. The WC unloaded a barrage of intercepting fire as we accelerated hard toward AV1, and then covered our approach by targeting the stations that could probably get a decent firing solution on us or the Xaviers when we launched them. We unloaded all four Xavier missiles as we got close enough to AV1 for collision alarms to start popping up, slowed for a split-second, nosed down after the missiles cleared in front of us, and then accelerated hard so that we should clear the underside of AV1 on an escape vector shielded from the side of the impact. We activated all four missiles which basically burst into the side of AV1 with what we hoped would be devastating results as we sped away dodging defensive fire on the other side. We picked up the Nova buoy launch signal from the WC as she broke apart under the close range weapons of AV1. She started to list and then was rammed by several of the bombers as it appeared they had lost their own flight controls, possibly after being hammered by the Winston Churchill. I looked for Knisse in the aftermath and didn't see her fighter anywhere on sensors. Cerb confirmed that she had gotten her up-close kiss with one of the bombers, which had sent it hurtling into the WC's fire and inevitably a collision with the WC that ended its existence.

I checked my sensors and found no more bombers in pursuit on my sensors. There were a few signs of bombers maybe floating out there, but nothing active. I checked for other fighters. I checked for other capital ships or vessels, drones or anything else. And then, as Mars rose above AV1 like a red sun, I realized I was utterly the only ship out here. Maybe the only human alive out here. Maybe the only thing that stood between that slowing monstrosity and annihilation of the human race. I felt like both a God and insignificant all at once as I sat, catatonic, contemplating that.

I shall be immortal.

## X.

After escaping from the defensive envelope of AV1's weapons, I circled and observed from a distance to see how the damage from the Xavier missiles had unfolded. It looked like they actually made contact with the hull, creating elongated gouges through to the interior of the ship, wreaking havoc across several systems and even spilling more of the aliens out into space. It felt good to know we could hurt them. Good to know that we'd taken some with us out here in our first alien battle in space! Cerb analyzed the damage, hull thickness, atmosphere, and an array of other data in order to have the most up-to-date information for our Nova buoy. This information would be profound if Earth was to truly defend itself. Not that there were any ships there to defend, but maybe something could be done. We were under no illusions now about going home. While we could, I didn't really see any reason to. He had an AI replica that would be on the buoy. I didn't really feel there was anything calling *me* back to Earth any longer. I would have loved to see my home and mountains and so many things one last time. But they're just that - Things. Objects to adore or touch, view or covet. Nothing more than objects, which won't have any bearing on my soul. Hell, a soul. It's a time to think about the implications of life and religion - but I'm not going to. I've got no stomach for either at this point, so I think I'll just push my chips in now, knowing I'm not a favorite, and see how the cards fall. I've got "a chip and a chair" as the poker romantics would tell you. And who knows, maybe fortune does favor the bold.

\*\*\*

"Cerb, is the buoy prepared?"
"Affirmative sir. Are you certain you want to launch before we attack?

You will look rather foolish, not to mention earning the ire of command and ridicule of AIs everywhere, having prematurely ejected your Nova buoy then returned alive. And who knows, maybe you'll discover some new tactic or way to attack them? It would be a shame to waste the opportunity to gather more data..."

"Launch the buoy, Cerb." We had planned to head straight for the impact zone of the Xavier missiles. We had a clear attack vector after AV1 cleared the bulk of debris, remains of a dead ship and thousands of lives: what was left of the Winston Churchill. The ejection of the buoy chimed throughout the module, an annoying sound that I felt was an awful racket to be the last thing someone hears as they die. Damn! And I thought I was sadistic. The question now was: do I fly like I'm dead? Or do I fly like I'm still alive?

We brought ourselves up to max safe acceleration, for such relatively small distances, and angled to pass below the monstrous ship. As long-range fire started coming in, we weaved upward toward the top then back toward the bottom. In short, we kept our front angle on our attack point and just rocked up and down in erratic motions so they couldn't really anticipate our location. I expended the rest of the Gauss cannon rounds, figuring they couldn't really miss something this large and I'd be able to actually watch their effect on something the size of AV1. Plus, it might keep some of the defensive fire off of us as their point defense would try to take out the projectiles.

We continued to approach the ship and we received little to no defensive fire. Perhaps we did more damage than I thought? Doubtful. Perhaps without the Xavier missiles they no longer feel threatened? That would just be tactically deranged on their part. And not even consistent. We had an ideal angle and I'd eventually do some damage, even if I just lased them with pulsed plasma fire for a while. I was starting to get defensive again, feeling like I was facing a cold and uncaring mountain.

"Just completed some analysis I was doing, sir. I think that ship is not a combat vessel. It's huge, yes, and has several weapons suites. But, unfortunately, the hull, speed, and arrangement of weapons leads me to believe that this is perhaps a colony or civilian-class vessel, perhaps meant to safely transport the large number of life readings I've detected within? The arrangement of weapons, as well..."

For about a second and a half, as I tuned out Cerb, I thought about how Earth's most devastating forces were just beaten, decidedly, by a *colony* ship? If I didn't feel disheartened before, I did now. What did they bring a colony ship for? Maybe it's a lost civilization looking for a home? Maybe it's an invasion force and they knew we didn't have the capacity to win? I spent several precious seconds pondering the implication of Cerb's data, and how I hadn't put it in the Nova Buoy. But I didn't have any more time to worry my little military mind about that, as Cerb coldly updated my Core view of AV1 with a sea of red dots – marking the small missile or drone-class objects AV1 had just unloaded as a wall right at us. It might have been a defensive barrier, given the energy readings coming off them, or maybe just a wall of anti-ship missiles? It didn't matter, as there was no way for us to avoid them given our relative speed and distance. All we could do is try to avoid a killing strike on us and ride it out. Interesting that I include Cerb when I think about "us" dying. I guess no one likes to think they're alone when they die. We rocked and bucked as explosions and bright beams of light danced across the view, shorting sensors, dazzling even my own eyes. We dove and zig'd, spun and slid, trying to keep from losing a main system or taking severe damage as I felt like the ship was being surgically dismantled around me. We started to lose pitch control....

I shall be immortal.

***

The stars were so lovely when I opened my eyes. It really shouldn't be any different than the inside of the Core, but it's unmistakeable when you use your own eyes. Even with these synthetic eyes I could tell the difference through the helmet. It was just so peaceful, floating along calmly. I wasn't twisting or moving at a high speed, it seemed, but rather just drifting along. I grabbed at my left wrist and activated the command device to see how much more damage I'd taken to my body or my suit. I didn't feel anything wrong, but then I wouldn't necessarily know if I were in shock or numb, of course. Bio scans actually looked clean excluding my charred back and bandaged leg. I didn't even have any new signs of physical trauma nor even debris attached to me. I could see it all around me, but not right here floating with me.

I activated the suit's stability system and had it start searching for any sensors to pick up what I could about the ship or any other new signals in the area. Data started to pour in, and I realized that I was still getting a feed from Cerb. He continued to gather as much information as possible before sending off our Nova data toward Earth. He always was stubborn for an AI. That also meant he must be stuck or damaged severely since we already sent it.

"Cerb, feed me your nav data and get me an orientation to any fleet signals."

Nothing happened.

"Cerb, feed me your nav data and get me an orientation to any fleet signals."

Still nothing. I started into a slow, slow roll sideways to try to visually spot any new information or see if there were any rescue vessels inbound. I could have been out for hours and drifted far away without even realizing it. But then I found it. The behemoth ship appeared slightly smaller now, maybe, but I could still see devastation where the Xaviers had impacted with the hull. She was there, silently hovering or moving away from me. She looked like I could reach out and touch her, but AV1 was so big, it would probably take hours to get to her with suit thrusters.

Some debris drifted past me at speed and I braced for the hit that would finally take me out. Javier Ortiz, great pilot and poker player extraordinaire, taken out by a piece of space debris. Probably from his own ship just to add insult to injury. Effing lovely. Yeah, I actually swore. Not really a reason to lay off now. But nothing hit me and I realized that maybe I should get out of the rain, metaphorically of course.

I looked for some large pieces of debris to make a sort of life raft or shield wall. I couldn't see anything in my immediate vicinity, so I checked the data on Cerb and the location marker of where the ship appeared to be. I found it, practically right below me, and tried to fire the attitude thrusters in an attempt to move toward what was left of my ship. They didn't seem to work properly, but I was able to fire one here or there and eventually figured out a pattern to actually get somewhere. After several minutes I was able to position and reposition and finally get my old body over to the fighter remains.

I watched from afar as I caught the occasional glimpse of a fireball or other explosion. Every time I hoped it was an alien survivor, exploding in space in some dazzling light show. I felt like a kid at fireworks marveling at every explosion. More likely though, there were other fighters out here still trying to save our species. Maybe I just hadn't been able to spot them earlier. Or, in a spiteful thought, it was the aliens systematically destroying life pods. Either way, it was like standing in front of an approaching storm - it hadn't rained yet and you could just watch the lightning strikes and the clouds collide overhead.

I shall be immortal.

\*\*\*

I found the show intoxicating as I drifted sideways toward the position of my fighter's remains, keeping it and the fireworks in view. As I approached, I noticed that the ship was casting a shadow toward the alien vessel AV1 which gave me a good reference on where the sun was so I could try to avoid more solar wind or rays, and also so I could avoid being blinded. It must have been ten more minutes of watching the storm before I got to my ship.

Systems were reporting "online" and I noticed that the Core had been practically dissected out of the center. The top and bottom pieces of the hull had been cut away, leaving just a sphere of lights which was the Core module itself. The hole in the middle looked like it belonged there, waiting for the peg to be put in the round hole. It still had some physical connections to the fighter, which would explain how it had minimal power and also how Cerb was still getting data though he hadn't launched the Nova buoy and seemed stuck in some sort of error. I tried connecting to the CAC wireless and suddenly my HUD activated the feed from my ship. Diagnostic data came pouring into my wrist module. Nav was down. Sensors were up but only on a few sides. Most everything else was down. I circled the ship, clumsily as I continued to figure out my booster patterns, looking at the damage. I had to get an idea of what the whole problem was in order to figure out if we were getting out of this one. For starters, I just need to get some of the ship working.

The damage didn't look so bad from the outside. This X-4 was a silver metal skin that looked like mercury floating in the void of space. I started with getting the core fully powered by the ship's powerplant. Luckily, with the minimal power it had, I was easily able to punch up schematics to figure out how to do what I needed. Once I had Cerb back on line, I was able to get the Core powered and then connected my suit to the Core's life support system. With the ship and the core activated, I ran diagnostics on my suit and verified that I was now running life support and some limited ship control through my suit commands. After a bit of recharging my suit, I headed back out and started to work on the sensors so I wouldn't fly blind.

My CAC flashed several messages, comm changes, status updates, and optical sensor reads. They were going to have to wait until I wasn't sitting out here in the void. But oh how I wanted to read them and feel like I was back in touch with people. Problem was, I already knew just from watching them come in that they were all older messages I hadn't received.

I backed off and took a few minutes to assess the damage and had difficulty from the shaded side of the ship. So I took the suit lights and tried to use them as a flashlight to light the ship.

The ship lit up like a blazing light bulb, temporarily blinding me as my eyes had adjusted to the darkness of space. If I'd had the ability I would have ducked! I noticed my shadow on the ship and hit my thrusters to spin around. Had someone out there already gotten here to rescue me?

I looked down at my data pad and the CAC feed as I slowly spun, stopping practically face-to-face with the nose of a vessel, clearly an alien bomber in design, with a large gash across its maw and filled with some sort of pink foam from front to two thirds of the way back. I have no idea how long it may have been quietly observing me. I waved reflexively in a "Hi" gesture, and the light energy dimmed somewhat from the alien nose, allowing me to make out the sleek curve of the bomber's fuselage. Energy crackled along its surface, visible to the eye at this range and looking like the ship was crawling with lightning or electrical discharges. What appeared to be turrets on the wings and even the nose cannon port sprang to life with the tell-tale signs of energy buildup.

I fired the suit controls to get back to my fighter, but I knew it was a futile gesture at this range and with nowhere to go. I made it to the fighter and swung around it like the proverbial sack of potatoes, to the opposite side of the fighter from the alien bomber. My mind raced to come up with a solution, but really all I could think about was checking the CAC for any hope for Paulsen or Knisse having made it out alive. And I realized I had a promise to keep by sending them my hand. I only needed a few seconds to do it, which turned into a furious minute or two as I tried to navigate the wrist-held command device. I sent out my poker information as promised, and in doing so kicked off an attempt to sync the device with current data. Now I had to wait a second before I could read anything.

I took the chance to peek over the top of the fuselage and search as best I could for the alien bomber. Nothing there. Maybe they left? Perhaps one good deed deserved another?

I started to run through the queue and found a message flagged private from Maria S Knisse's private account. Damn! This message actually had, during the battle, rolled back through Canada, through to Earth, out to Canada, and out to me.

I had trouble viewing it with the light on me and moved a little so I could change the direction that the Sun's reflection was hitting the wrist-comm so it would stop blinding me. And there she was, behind me again, lit up like a Christmas tree but just sitting there, observing.

I turned toward it again as it slowly moved downward, eclipsing the sunlight that had been reflecting off my comm device. The lack of sound out here and the visual of the ship eclipsing the sun and watching me was eerie in a way I'd never really experienced. I wasn't going anywhere right now, and I didn't even have a weapon. I stared at them defiantly for a few minutes. Then, as they did nothing I decided I was going to read my message from Knisse.

It had six words. Words that made me laugh as the alien vessel finally started toward me with a feral leap, weapons lit up like stars in the sky. Sometimes you don't have the winning hand.

[Hey, mister Immortal. Pocket Threes. - MKnisse]

***Catalino Tolejano, II** is a Martial Art hacking, Cartoon-watching, Computer nerd-ing, Comic-Con-ing, Triathlon-scrambling, Wedding officiating, Sci-fi geek-ing, RPG-ing, Lawn mowing, M&M collecting, Video gaming, House fixing, Stargazing, Weapon flailing, Self-inflicting, Toy collecting, Uber-dork extraordinaire! All rolled into a Miami Dolphins fan trapped in Wisconsin."*

# Honor Among Traitors

*Patrick A. Waldoch*

"Capt, this new MEGS package you got for the Bootlegger is really freaking sweet. I can easily make out the Half Moon on the edge of this debris field. They are just entering the Lagrange point now."

"I'm glad you like the new sensors package Mr. Colmes, now please keep an eye on them and sing out when they get within a 45 degree cone of our bow, and for God's sake don't go active on the radar."

"Hey! That was only once and it was due to combat damage Captain!" Colmes cries out.

"Sure, ok, Mr. Colmes. Back to your display, please."

Sometimes that boy drives me nuts. He's a pretty good operator for our multi-energy-gravitic sensors, or MEGS, and he's probably right about the combat damage at the time, but if the Half Moon saw us now, she could easily turn around, head out of the Lagrange point, and fold away before we could engage her. I'm not losing this ship. We need the prize money the Confeds will pay for her and her cargo.

"So, how did you get that package anyway?" asks my new 3rd officer Marty Callahan as he's walking onto the bridge. Good ears on him. Heard our conversation from around the bulkhead.

"That cash game when we met with the Durban brothers for supplies and refit. There was a nice gentleman arms dealer at the poker game they were hosting who called out a re-raise to my raise before he even realized he didn't have the money. He offered to put up an 'acquired...'", as I sign double-fingered quotes, "... military sensors refit kit and some extra railgun and torpedo ordnance that he

**123**

was going to sell, but if he left the game he'd have to forfeit the hand, so I said I'd accept it at 10 percent of its value."

"At 10 percent value?"

"Why, yes. He wanted 50 percent and that value would have been enough to easily double my raise. But I could see he was starting to sweat and all it took to convince him was a little girlish twirl of auburn," as I shake my head a little to send my hair down my shoulder, "a flash of baby blues," as I exaggerate blinking my eyes, "and just let my zipper on my jacket slink down a few extra notches."

Marty laughs at the show. "And I suppose you won the hand in the end?"

"Oh, yes. Seven-four off-suit. Matched up with a pair of sevens on the flop and a four on the turn. He thought his two pairs of aces and sevens were gonna hold. Seven-four off-suit, best hand in the game."

"Apparently. What happened to the old sensors suite? We didn't sell it, I assume, otherwise the quarter master would have told me it was gone." Being my logistics officer Marty would also know if it was put into storage.

"I gave it to engineering to play around with, wanted the Chief to try a few things out."

"Like what?"

"Captain's Privilege." I replied. A girl's gotta have some secrets.

"Yes, sir."

"'Yes, ma'am' will do. You're still relatively new here, but while I run this ship with a near-military discipline, I don't abide the silly tradition of calling every female officer 'sir.' I see no need to 'sir' an officer simply to be 'gender neutral.' I have mammary glands and ovaries. That generally makes one a female and females are called ma'am." I had a hard enough time coming up the ranks in the Unitary Spacial Navy's old-boys club. My ship, my rules. Advancement is by merit and skill alone.

"Yes, ma'am!" Marty replies with enthusiasm. Eager beaver. Good. Maybe he'll last.

---

About ten minutes later, "Captain! The Half Moon is within our front 45 degree arc and is changing her bearing. She's heaving to her starboard and has now put her stern to us and is diving roughly 30 degrees in relation to our elliptic plane."

"Excellent. That's the proper course for the Half Moon to reach the habitat." The Damocles system's gas giant, designated as Damocles-4, has a fairly large moon, designated as D4-7, but with a ton of asteroid debris at the L4 and L5 Lagrange points in the Damocles-4 and D4-7 orbital system. There are five Lagrange points in every defined orbiting mass pair, like a star and one of its planets, or a planet and one of its moons. They are points of neutral gravity where the gravitational pull between the two objects are canceled out. L1 and L2 points are small and are really near the smaller orbiting body. L3 points are nearly the exact opposite side of the orbit of the smaller body around the larger one. Its the L4 and L5 where things can get fun. Those points are roughly 60 degrees before and after the smaller body in it's orbit. But they tend to be a bit 'fuzzy' and you generally get an area of space that's gravity neutral or close enough to it that a hyper-fold engine can't make fold into or out of that area. They also tend to collect debris, from small dust like Jupiter in the Earthspace to larger asteroids, just like D4-7's two points have. Great place for natural rocks to make habitats from and work on them with out having to drag a rock from an asteroid belt, but damn tricky to get in and out of quickly. But it also means the prizes can't get away as easily.

"Chief-of-the-Ship, please secure us from silent running and sound general quarters. WEPS this is the conn. Have the forward tubes loaded for EM munitions and the rail guns primed but both them and the plasma turrets on standby. I want that ship intact and repairable when this is all over, Mr. Sann." More prize money that way but harder than just hulling the ship and picking out the cargo from the debris. My Weapons Officer Joao "Gunny" Sann knows exactly what I want and how to run the guns and not over do it. Sometimes I swear he can read minds. Maybe he can and that's how he beats me in sparring practice so regularly.

"COMMS, give my compliments to the Deck Master and tell her I'd be pleased to have her prep Timothy and his Booze squadron pilots to be ready to launch at my command. We shouldn't need the fighters, but just in case."

"Aye aye, Captain."

At this point the bridge is just a-buzz with activity as orders are being carried out over the entire ship, getting the Bootlegger into a state of combat readiness. The crew knows their jobs. They also know that the prize money for the Half Moon and her cargo is worth quite a tidy sum. While many things may motivate a person, profit is usually one of the big ones. While the bridge is busy, I patch my ships comms station to engineering.

"Engineering, get me my chief engineer." I start getting possessive of everyone before we go into combat. Mothering instinct? Ha.

"Finley here, Captain. Engines are primed and at top efficiency. Power systems and control are ready to go, and I have damage repair crews ready to deploy if needed."

"Good, Daniel. Was the package deployed successfully?"

"Yes, ma'am. Just after we arrived."

"Very good. Bridge out. Miss Haggerty, move us out at one-quarter power right behind the target. Stay directly behind her so WEPS has a line up on her engines for the torps shot. That class of ship doesn't have any decent view ports to the rear and they shouldn't see us until its almost too late. Mr. Colmes, please continue passive monitoring."

"Aye aye, Cap."

We've been under silent-running protocol for a few hours with basically only life support running and passive MEGS. The bridge crew is itching for some action. A quick glance through the internal security cameras shows the rest of the crew in a similar state.

"Conn, WEPS. We'll be in optimal firing solution in 30 seconds."

"Excellent, WEPS." Forward view port feed shows we're slotted in behind the Half Moon and closing. "Ok, MEGS, give WEPS an active firing solution sweep."

"Pinging with radar and laser designators now, Captain."

"Conn, this is WEPS. I have a final firing solution. Ready to fire."

"Captain, MEGS! New contact! 180 elliptical planar, 200 dorso-ventral planar, and I have active ranging radar coming from her! ID'ing the ship now."

"Damn! They are right behind us! MEGS, electronic countermeasures NOW! WEPS, get all systems hot and ready! COMMS, get me the hanger deck, then engineering." No one was supposed to know we were here!

Another voice sings out on the Bootlegger's bridge. "Miss Haggerty, punch it! Chief! Get the aft torpedo room to load EX torps and be ready to fire soonest at the direction of WEPS, and have the ventral particle cannons get a bearing on the contact," hollers my 1st officer, Mr. Samuels, to the Chief-of-the-Ship, as he's just returned to the bridge and started strapping himself into his station.

"Mr. Colmes, I need information! What have you got for me?!" We can live or die by information or lack of it. I've got a sinking feeling about this situation.

"She's a destroyer class ship, Captain, squawking as the Unitary Ship Prometheus. She's bigger than us, and her guns are bearing right on us. She popped up from behind our own hiding spot. She must have been there the whole time under silent running. How'd she know exactly were we'd be, Captain?"

Sinking feeling confirmed. "Damn good question, which we'll figure out later. First we gotta HAVE a later that doesn't include us captured or killed."

"Incoming transmission. It's the Prometheus," my signals officer, Yvette pipes up. Petite little blond thing, but a set of lungs that can scream over any noise on the bridge and yet not actually be yelling.

"Put it to my station please."

My station's comscreen comes alive with the face of a man I've never met before. He's somewhat handsome, dark haired and clean shaven, as most Unitary officers are.

"To the pirate ship Bootlegger: This is the USN ship Prometheus. We have you under our guns and you are ordered to stand down. You have been observed in an attempted attack on a Unitary merchant freighter. Stand down and prepare to be boarded."

"Prometheus, this is Captain Marlene Pritchard of the private yacht Bootlegger. I don't know how you found us or knew of my plans but I have absolutely no intention of standing down and turning over my ship to you. I've spent plenty of time on Unitary ships in my time as a Unitary Space Navy officer and I don't plan on spending any more time on one."

"Captain Pritchard, I outgun you by half, and we're both trapped in this debris field inside the Lagrange point. You can't get out and towards Damocles' gravity well to fold out of here before I pound you to scrap. Stand down and save your crew."

Hidden from the Prometheus, a text message from Mrs. Yvette scrolls across my personal control screen, [Captain, I have both the hanger deck and engineering on the line.] I type back [Tell Chief Finley to activate the package in mode 2 now and to tell Deckmaster Kincade to have the fighters stand by ready to launch.]

As I direct my attention quickly back to the Prometheus' captain before he thinks I'm not giving him my complete attention and in a more soothing and reasonable sounding tone of voice. "Captain...?"

"Heward."

"Captain Heward." [Launch fighters] I text over to Mrs. Yvette. "You are under the misunderstanding that you have the upper hand here."

Over in the background of the commline to Captain Heward, I hear "Contact! Active emissions dead astern! Something's got a lock on us! Large destroyer signature, running match now. Torpedoes inbound from the stern!!"

"Captain, seems you're a bit busy at the moment with my friend the Bottle o' Rum at your tail. Oh, just to make your life interesting at your Admiralty hearing when they review your after action report, let me introduce you to some more headaches - my fighters."

The captain seems just a bit preoccupied at the moment as the two torpedoes from the "Bottle o' Rum" slam into his engines and his lights flicker on his command bridge. Wait til he sees fighters in the sky.

"Fighters? From the Bootlegger?" Captain Heward seems to have forgotten he has an open comm call to me while he's paying attention to his officers relaying him information.

"Yes Captain Heward, fighters. Aren't they a pretty sight to behold?"

"A Corsair class frigate doesn't have a hanger bay let alone one for fighters!?"

"Mine does. Cost me a pretty penny too. Goodbye Captain." I cut the transmission. Paid a pretty penny alright for the hanger bay and a few other modifications. Of course I lost a quarter of my cargo space, the VIP luxury quarters deck and some escape pods but it was well worth it. Besides the Unitary government paid for it all in a manner of speaking.

"MEGS, active CIAR plots to my station now." I don a pair of augmented reality glasses and get a 3D plot in front of me in with a 3rd person view of the Bootlegger and the locations of other ships, probable locations of contacts, current vectors, etc. Much easier to visualize the combat sphere around the Bootlegger but I've known some people who get lost in the AR world and forget there is a real combat situation going on.

Max cries out again. "Two torps launched from Prometheus. She's bearing away from us towards the probable location of the Bottle o' Rum, but I don't have a return ping nor a visual on the Rum yet."

Nor will you.

"Conn, WEPS. Point defense lasers engaging torps." Gunny Sann pipes to the bridge.

Good man. Made the transition to space from being a ground pounder like he was born to it. We're gonna need it. He knows how to handle his weapon crews like they are an extension of him.

"Bootlegger, this is Booze lead. We're clear and headed over to harass the Prometheus." Since they don't have fighters of their own, they will have to depend on their point defense lasers and particle cannons to engage them. Neither of which is as good as another space fighter.

"All hands brace for impact!" Sann broadcasts over the entire ship.

I see a small red line trace towards us from the Prometheus and impact our main thruster cluster, and as that happens, the entire ship shakes and a dull thud of the explosion reverberates throughout the ship. The internal gravitational compensators dull a portion of the impact on the crew but everyone is shaken and dazed for a few seconds.

"Miss Haggerty, there is a large rock at..." I instinctively reach out to the CIAR's display of a decent sized asteroid trying to get it's vector details and realize I didn't put on my AR gloves. "Dammit! Its roughly 45 by 45 from us...up and to the right! Just get us around that sucker ASAP!" as I start pulling on my gloves.

"I see it. Moving us there now."

I manually comm engineering, the Signals station is going to be busy directing damage control crews, "Engineering, Report!"

"Main thrusters took a beating, we're about two thirds capable thrust but I'm not sure how long we could sustain that for. Also lost some control vectoring on the starboard side of our engines. Armor's peeled back over there like an overripe banana, and I've already lost two crew members in that area."

"Keep those engines up and get me whatever you can back on

the starboard vectoring controls." And if we don't all join them in the next few minutes, I'll say a short prayer for those crew members' souls.

"Aye aye, Captain."

Damn, two dead already. And the Half Moon is effectively gone. Someone's gonna have to pay for this.

Besides just me.

I lean over towards my First officer. "Johnny, we need to get the hell out of here, soonest. I see we got two main options here: either we go out the way we came, running right past the Prometheus, or we try to plot and pick our way out of this. I say we take a run past the Prometheus while she's pointing away now looking for a destroyer that doesn't exist."

"The Rum doesn't exist?" my third officer butts in.

"That's right, Mr. Callahan. That was our old MEGS transmitter rigged to look like a large destroyer and hooked up with two torpedoes in a bastardized launcher." Always keep an Ace up your sleeve if you can. I once read in an old classic book, "If you ain't cheatin' you ain't trying hard enough." Of course the author was talking about hunting monsters, but it still applies.

"Captain!" Marty pipes up. "We can't go up against that ship! Even with her engines damaged and our fighters, she's more than a match for us! We should pick our way through the debris field and find another way out!"

"Captain, I disagree. We have maybe one opportunity to get a shot at the Prometheus in the next few minutes before she stops looking for the Bottle o' Rum and turns back and comes for us. We hit her hard while she's got her backside towards us we can damage her main thrusters enough to slow her down and get away. Yeah, we're gonna take some serious particle cannon fire on the way past but if we go picking around this debris field looking for a way out, either the debris will get us because we're going too fast, or the Prometheus will pound our thrusters until we can't move anymore. Then we're easy pickings. Remember that bounty on us is for dead or alive."

"I concur, Mr. Samuels. Miss Haggerty! New course! Back the way we came! All available acceleration. Pass the Prometheus from under her as she currently sits." I key open the comm to WEPS station. "WEPS, this is the conn. Load up the forward tubes for an attack. Use penetrators. I don't expect them to make it to the target at this close a range and with little maneuvering or acceleration but I want more targets for them to worry about. But I want those rail guns to blow the hell out of the ass end of that destroyer just before we're about to pass her or we won't make it out of this alive! Have all the cannons fire as the guns bear, point defense too. We need to pound that ship as hard as we can to give us our window to escape them. "

"As ordered, Captain," replies Gunny.

"But Captain! We won't survive against the Prometheus! We must run away!" Marty leaps out of his station and runs right up and grabs my shoulders to attempt to make his point.

"MR. CALAHAN! Back to your station and direct those supplies to the damage control crews, NOW!"

"Captain, you must see reason! I can't let you do this!" he continues to scream at me while I catch his right hand dropping to his sidearm.

While, I'm not exactly a muscular woman, I did go through USN hand to hand training, and between Gunny and Chief Nate they don't let me slack on my combat practice. I quickly use my left arm to sweep his arm away from his gun and add some palm heel blows to his groin, solar plexus and then his throat while I step into him and sweep his right leg. He goes down quickly with a loud THUD on the bridge's deck.

"Chief-of-the-Ship, would you have Mr. Callahan removed from my bridge and placed in the brig, then have Midshipman Garrett come up from stores and assume Mr. Callahan's duties please?"

"Yes, ma'am! Lets go, sir." While the Chief may be a man in his upper years with gray hair everywhere, he's got a body like a trim wrestler. He hoists Callahan like he was just a bag of laundry and turns back to me. "Pretty good, ma'am, but you dropped your left after sweeping his arm away. We'll practice some more after we're out of this trap." He proceeds to take Marty and dump him outside the bridge to the waiting guards there.

"Yes, Sensei." I reply with a little nod, mimicking a bow. The rewards of training. More training. And bruises.

"Captain. I have us lined up with the Prometheus and we'll pass her in a minute."

"WEPS, fire the torpedoes. Ready the rail guns. Signals, tell Stormbringer to get ready to have his squadron follow us out of the theater and to dock once we're clear of the Prometheus."

The CIAR shows two tracks for our torpedoes leaving our position and heading out to the Prometheus and then a pair of cones come from the back of the Prometheus showing her active point defense systems. Being a larger ship than us they can have at least two, sometimes three, laser defense turrets in any major arc in as close as 200 meters. Since we didn't fire our torps from a few kilometers away, they don't have enough time to speed up and maneuver against incoming point defense fire. Sure enough, they get one almost right away.

"Captain, the Prometheus has halted all forward movement

and is starting to heel around. I think Captain Heward has just figured out that the Rum isn't real. She's firing two torps of her own at us but we'll be in minimum distance of those torps' safeties before they can get to us...I think." Johnny hollers out towards me, there ain't nothing guaranteed in combat.

"Conn, WEPS, we're in optimum firing position for the rails!"

"FIRE! FIRE!"

"Everyone brace for multiple impacts!" shouts Johnny over the ship-wide comm.

One of the torpedoes from the Prometheus' rear tubes slams Bootlegger and we get rewarded with a big explosion that jolts everyone across the ship. We just made it under the range safety distance but apparently Captain Heward was smart enough to disable the range safety before firing. Some things just don't change, like torpedo tactics. Deep space, deep water, its still the same. The bow gets hit by the second torpedo on the starboard side and again the ship shakes and buckles as we absorb the damage, but luckily that one seems to have glanced us some so we didn't get the full fury of the warhead explosion.

Just then my CIAR display flickers for a minute along with all the bridge station displays. But it's not due to the torpedo, but from the two ventrally mounted rail guns on my ship firing. The magneto-gravitic accelerators on that gun accelerate a half kilogram slug to about 0.0001 the speed of light as it leaves the gun. Usually only found on larger ship-of-the-line sized battle-cruisers and the like, I had a twin launcher system modified to fit along the belly of the Bootlegger. The problem is it plays merry hell with ship's systems for a brief second as they fire. In this case I'm firing both at one time. Launching two slugs to that velocity sucks a huge amount of power, thus the disruption. And if the power plant is down, we can't fire them from batteries. However when they hit, they impart a massive amount of kinetic energy that just blows past the gravitic space dust repelling field of a ship and impacts with a force nearly as large as a small tactical nuke. More than my torps can do since I can't get any real nuclear warheads on a regular basis. It's a great surprise factor. Now even a small corvette warship can survive a round or two of an up close rail gun but the damage is more than enough to cripple it. A ship the size of the Prometheus is gonna know it's been hit hard.

As our counter-fire rail-guns slams into the Prometheus' backside I see my display is showing me her thrusters are definitely damaged badly and maybe out of action for the time being. Maybe we got lucky and the rail-gun rounds penetrated far enough into the ship that we damaged her power core. In any case, we're moving past the Prometheus and trading off full broadsides of particle cannon fire and everything else. Hell, I'll shoot spitwads at this point if someone told me they were ready to fire! We get the hell beat out of us as we pass each other as she's got more guns to bear on us, but we're still accelerating and we'll get cover from her guns in this debris field as we start to make our way out the way we came.

"CONTACT! Torpedo inbound! Radiological detector on the MEGS is showing..a tactical nuke?!"

I key up weapons again. "WEPS! You see the inbound nuke?! Knock that thing out of my space now or we're dead!" Ok this just isn't fair. When the hell'd they start passing out tac nukes on destroyers?! That's just a wee bit more damage than my rail guns can produce.

"I'm on it, Captain." I get as a comm message from Stormbringer in Booze one.

"Stormbringer, ARE YOU INSANE?!? Get the hell out of the rear arc or you'll get hit by the cannon fire or the torp's blast!" shouts my first officer. Those two go way back. Like grade school back.

"Johnny, relax. I got this.. oops! Ok. I'm Ok. Just a little bit more.. BINGO!" and on the rear view port feed I see an explosion as Booze lead shoots down the torpedo with his guns.

"Tim, why the hell didn't you at least use a missile to shoot that thing down?" Johnny asks him over the comm.

"Oh, well I wasn't sure it would hit. I knew my guns would hit it."

"Damn show off."

"And you know it!"

He's gonna be an insufferable prick for the next few months and is probably gonna want a bonus on the next prize share out. I think I can easily convince the crew's bonus prize board to give it to him on the account of him saving our collective butts.

"Booze squadron, combat docking is authorized. Get in here so we can get out of this place fast."

"Aye aye, ma'am."

---

We're safe now. After getting out of the debris field and moving towards Damocles-4 we're close enough to the gravity field of the planet to make a space fold to deeper Confed space. After I tidy up this business I'll find us somewhere to hold up for some repairs. Right now I have everyone except the standard watches mustered on the hanger deck area.

"Everyone gather around for disciplinary witness!" cries out Chief-of- the-Ship Green. That call is just a formality as everyone is already here.

Callahan is shackled hands and feet and is the center of a ring of the ships crew of just over 200, minus the crew on duty and the twenty one of those we lost getting out.

"Mr. Callahan. The ship's articles say traitors will be shot and spaced if the traitor's action causes bodily harm to any member of the crew. Seems the crew would just prefer to lynch you and I'm inclined to let them but Deck Master Kincade told me she doesn't want to have to clean up the blood from the hanger deck."

"But Captain! I know I got a bit agitated on the bridge and I'm sorry for that but how does that make me a traitor?"

"That didn't make you a traitor. The fact you sold us out to the USN makes you a traitor. The Prometheus knew exactly where we were going to be in that debris field. The only people that knew my plan for capturing the Half Moon at our last port of call were you, Mr. Samuels, and Chief Finley -- and of course myself. Second Officer McBride being off ship until the last minute, she was therefore not privy to the plans ahead of time."

"So it could be any of them! I'm not a traitor!" He starts crying nervously.

"Yes but Mr. Samuels and Chief Finley were also the only ones privy to my plan for construction of the "Bottle o' Rum" decoy at that same port of call. Had either of them been the traitor the Prometheus would have known of the decoy, instead of falling for the deception and getting distracted for a few minutes in combat looking for a larger ship. Considering they were in position well before we were and hidden well, they would have been watching more closely with a drone or two for the decoy placement."

"But.."

"But what, Mr. Callahan? I'm guessing you're not who you said you really are when you signed on two months ago."

Looking dejected at first, but then straightening up a bit, Callahan replies. "No. I'm with USN Intelligence. I was sent to infiltrate your ship and help bring you to justice. I've failed my mission obviously but I don't regret any of my actions. Your kind has..."

BANG! He falls down in front of my still smoking vintage Colt 1911 pistol with a bullet hole in his head. I don't want to hear his self righteous bullcrap. The sins I've committed are nothing compared to the sins of the Unitary Nations government. Oppression, indentured servitude that's no more than slavery, raping of colony worlds and those who live there to feed the inner Earthsphere planets. No, I'm no saint, I'm a mercenary and maybe a traitor to the Unitary government, but not to myself and to my crew.

My first officer takes charge of the situation. "Someone space this trash, please."

Coming back to reality I glance over to Johnny and eye him with a look of gratitude as I muster some steel back in my voice, "Chief Green, dismiss the crew."

*Patrick A. Waldoch*

*Patrick A. Waldoch* is a Computer System-Network BOfH *(look it up) with too many expensive hobbies. Between motorcycle track days (when he can scrounge up the cash for track fees), practical shooting sports (when he can scrounge up the cash for ammunition) and his girlfriend (when he can scrounge up the cash for dinners and sparkly things for her. - just kidding she's the best!) He also plays RPG's regularly. At Gencon you might know him as one of the dwarves from Bad Apple Inc,- Grumpy.*

*If you read writing blogs, watch podcasts, attend workshops, and talk to authors – it becomes pretty clear that writing is far more often a skill learned through study, hard work, and practice, rather than simply a natural-born talent possessed by all authors.*

***AuthorsRising.com*** *is a place for up-and-coming authors to come together and collaborate on stories, learn from each other, and hone their skills. Authors Rising, LLC publishes collections of those stories, on behalf of the authors involved.*

*If you'd like to be a part of one of our books, and are willing to work hard, meet deadlines, and take & give honest, well-intentioned feedback from your fellow authors, come check us out.*

*We'd love to have you be a part of the community.*